Dedication

To my family. Always.

Christmas for Commitmentphobes

By Rhoda Baxter

Get a free novella when you sign up to my newsletter.

Details are at the end of this book.

Enjoy *Christmas for Commitmentphobes.* ☺

Chapter 1

Lara clicked onto the last slide. "In conclusion," she said. "I think we would be able to provide you with a bespoke logistics solution that would cut your fuel costs and reduce downtime between stages, saving you both time and money." She smiled at the room.

Her audience, four men, did not respond for a moment. They caught each other's eyes.

"Have you got any questions?"

One of the men leaned back in his chair and hooked his thumb in his belt. "I have a few questions about the software," he said.

"Go ahead."

He raised an eyebrow at her. "No offence love, but it's quite technical."

Lara forced down her instinctive response. "The research the software is based on is, is mine. I often instruct the technical guys. I should be able to help." She drew a breath. "If I can't answer, I can certainly get you the information from someone who can."

He exchanged a glance with his colleague, the corner of his mouth twitching. "It's about the way it tracks how long the boys have been driving and logs it. How do you ensure it's secure and compliant with GDPR? You know, the general data protection rules."

She knew what GDPR was. She also knew that the software was processing the data only for the purposes of allowing the drivers to carry out their jobs. She had already explained their data safety protocols. There was no real conflict here. The fact that these people assumed she would be confused by any of this annoyed her beyond measure. She had helped design this software. Technically, her role was fundraising and coordination, but as a co-founder, this was as much her product at her colleague Toby's.

Still, sexist clients were part and parcel of this business. She stuck on a smile and launched into an explanation. It might have been a tiny bit more technical than necessary, but he had wanted technical.

"Does that allay your fears?" she said at the end.

"Er..." The first guy looked at his colleagues, one of them was nodding, while the other two seemed to have glazed over.

"Basically," she said. "We don't interfere with your employee management software. The limited amount of information that comes to our system is kept secure. There is no issue with GDPR."

There was a silence in the room. Lara could tell how this was going to go. They were interested in the results, but would feel more comfortable if a man had delivered it. There was nothing wrong with the product. If Toby had delivered the pitch, they'd be shaking hands and inviting him to the pub by now, but Toby was off on paternity leave and the new sales person didn't start until January, so she had to do it by herself. She could tell that she wasn't going to be able to swing the decision now, so she went for plan B.

"It's a fairly big decision, so why don't I email you the information and the quotation and you can take a bit of time to think about it. Get back to me next week?" It took effort not to grit her teeth. "You'll probably have to talk to my colleague Toby, rather than me, but I'm sure he'll be able to process this for you."

It was nearly Christmas. These guys would probably leave it until after the holiday anyway, so she'd chase them next month. By which time, Toby would be back from pat leave and he could do that thing where he made the client laugh and then somehow closed the deal.

The shift in the mood of the room was subtle, but they seemed happy with that. It was only a little white lie. She opened her folder and extracted a few sheets. "I'll just leave you copies of the projections." She slid the papers to each of the men, then quietly packed up her laptop.

"Have you got far to go to get home, love?" said another man. They had all called her 'love' so far. It was so irritating.

"London," she said. "So a few hours on the train."

"Doesn't look nice out there," he nodded towards the window. It was already getting dark, even though it was only four o'clock.

Lara peered out of the window and saw swirling white flakes. "It's snowing?" Oh great.

TILLY LOOKED OUT OF the window at the motorway signs and wondered how to say no to her friend Diane's suggestion without being rude.

"Why don't you take a bit of time to think about it? Get back to me after Christmas," Diane said, as she took the jeep into the right lane.

"I dunno…" She was sitting in the front of Diane's dad's jeep. The back of the vehicle was crammed full of Diane's Christmas stuff, one small Christmas tree and Tilly's backpack. "It's not really the sort of thing I do. I do more painting than sculpting. Anyway, I feel uncomfortable working to a brief you wrote specifically for someone else's skillset."

Diane sighed. "I know, I know. But you could make it your own. All it said on the proposal was that it would be a landscape sculpture. We submitted the brief with Don's drawings, but given the exceptional circumstances, they'll let us substitute the artist, so we should be able to substitute your style for his. I've seen your stuff. It would work." Diane threw a glance across to her. "And you did say that your mum complained that she hasn't seen much of you. You'd be based in England. You could go home more often."

Tilly laughed. "Yeah. Mum would like that. Not sure how well I'd cope though."

"Aw. Your mum's lovely," said Laine. She scowled out of the window. "Bugger. It's snowing or sleeting or something."

In the yellow motorway glow, white flakes splattered against the windshield faster than the wipers could clear it off. Diane turned them up a notch.

"If the weather is going to slow you down, just drop me off in the next town and I'll get a train to this place." Tilly got out her phone and started looking up Trewton Royd.

"Don't be silly. We're in a four wheel drive. There's nothing that we can't get through in this old girl." Diane gave the steering wheel a pat. "Besides, I'm not going to abandon you somewhere just because the weather is crap. What kind of a friend would that make me?"

"A ... fair weather friend?"

Diane glanced over at her and laughed. "That's a terrible joke."

Tilly grinned.

"I've missed you, I really have," said Diane.

"Missed you too, mate."

"No, I mean, genuinely. I love that you want to travel the world and stuff, but dear god, I miss having you around."

Tilly smiled. "Aww. That's ... nice to know." The search results popped up on her phone. "This pub looks nice," She said. "Let's hope my brother resists the temptation to lecture me about staying in one place."

Diane didn't take her eyes off the road. "How's Vinnie getting there? I hope he's not driving his little car in this weather."

"He said he's taking his girlfriend's private car or something." Tilly shook her head. "She's some sort of internet millionaire person."

"He always did like his high maintenance girlfriends," said Diane.

"This one isn't high maintenance, according to Vinnie. Even if she was, she'd be able to pay for it herself. She can't drive, though. Hence the car and driver." Tilly settled back in her seat. "Mum's hoping he'll stay with this one. She really likes her."

"Your mum likes everyone."

"No she doesn't. She *pretends* she likes everyone." She tilted her head and looked at the darkness sliding past outside. The chances of her mum approving of someone she brought home would be pretty slim. Her parents said they were okay with her being gay, but every time she went home, there were comments about her lifestyle. It didn't take a genius to figure out what the problem was. She had never bothered to take a girlfriend home to meet them. What was the point?

"Tracey, that's Vinnie's girlfriend - Her aunt owns the pub we're going to be staying at over Christmas," Tilly continued. "I'm really looking forward to this. Not just seeing Vinnie, obviously, but you know, proper English Christmas. I haven't had a good old fashioned roast dinner in ages. Vinnie says the village is proper idyllic too."

"And just think, if you took over Don's part of the arts council grant ... you could see Vinnie all the time," Diane said. "It's tied to the 'northern powerhouse' region, so you'd be up this way anyway."

"Diane..."

"Seriously, Tilly. Why not? It's paid work. You can definitely do a good job of it. What are you afraid of?"

"I'm not afraid of anything," said Tilly. She folded her arms. "I just don't want to rush into anything."

"It's a job, mate. Not marriage. You do it for a year. It's not a long term commitment. We all know you don't get on with those."

"Don't you start. I get enough of that from mum... and the big brothers."

"Maybe they have a point?"

"Hmm."

For a few minutes there was silence, apart from the hum of the engine and whump, whump of the wipers. Tilly stared sulkily out of the window. This was why she'd stayed away last Christmas. The holiday seemed to bring out the worst in people when it came to judging her. She liked having no ties. What was so wrong with that?

Chapter 2

When Lara arrived at the train station, it was full of angry people.

"What's going on?" she asked, not really expecting an answer from anyone.

"All the trains have been bloody cancelled, haven't they?" said a woman with what looked like a million shopping bags. "I just want to get home." She pointed to the departures boards. All of which said 'Delays expected' on them.

Lara looked across the crowded waiting area. There were people everywhere. The platforms were full too. If a train did arrive, there was no way she'd manage to force herself on to it. She pulled the collar up on her coat, stepped back outside into the biting cold and phoned the office.

"There's been some sort of major accident," said Katrin, the administrator. "All the trains are suspended."

Lara shivered. "How long before it gets going again?" Her coat was designed to look good and maybe cope with a slight drizzle. It wasn't able to cope with snow and wind that seemed to be made of knives.

"I don't know. I'm trying taxi firms on the other phone, but they're all ringing out. The weather isn't helping much," said Katrin. "I don't think there will be any trains tonight. Taxi isn't looking too hopeful either."

"How am I going to get home?" Lara wailed. Her stomach growled, reminding her that she hadn't eaten since about eleven o'clock. "Katrin!"

"Okay, okay, calm down," said Katrin. "Let me see if I can book you into a hotel for the night. Things will be better in the morning and at least you'll be safe and warm in the meantime."

"Thank you." Lara hugged her laptop bag to her and waited. She looked around for somewhere to sit, but there wasn't anywhere. There was a spare bit of wall she could lean on though. She made towards it. A mother with a small child by the hand got to it just as she did. Lara took one look at the child and moved out of the way. The mother gave her a grateful half smile and got the child to sit down, with her back against the wall. Lara shuffled away.

Two men walked past, swearing. "The whole ******* thing's cancelled 'cause of the ******* weather," one of them said. "All we can do is go to the pub, really." They were both wearing t-shirts with the union flag emblazoned on them. One of them looked up and caught sight of Lara. She hurriedly looked away.

"Katrin? Any luck?"

There was the sound of furious typing at the other end of the line. "Gnh," said Katrin.

"That doesn't sound good." A terrible sense of foreboding was starting to build in Lara's mind.

"There aren't any rooms in Huddersfield. It looks like there's some sort of convention or something and the whole place is full. I'm looking further afield, hang on."

"Convention," Lara muttered. The closer she looked at some of the people around her, the more the sense of dread increased. Most of them were regular people, carrying bags.

There were quite a lot of heavily tattooed, Union Jack wearing types though. Suddenly, she was very aware of her non-whiteness. She wished she had a hoodie or something she could pull up.

"Gotcha. One second Lara. I think I've found somewhere."

The phone line crackled as Katrin muted the line. Suddenly, Lara felt very very alone. She walked over to the taxi rank. There was a huge queue. Bugger. Her stomach rumbled again. There was a shop a little way down the road. Food. She should get something to eat. She started down the road towards the shop.

As she reached it, Katrin came back on the line. "Okay, got one. There's a B&B, a few miles away. You'll have to take a taxi there. I've sent the location to your phone. Okay, I'm going to see if I can get you a taxi or a car or something. I'll call you back."

"No. Katrin don't-" Too late, she'd hung up. Lara lowered her phone. "Damn." The phone had a new map location marker on it. Fine. She'd just have to wait a few moments for Katrin to find her a car. In the meantime, it looked like she was stuck in Yorkshire for the night. Snow settled on her hair and cold slid down her back. She looked further down the road. There were more shops. Although it was dark, it wasn't exactly late and the shops were still open. Right. She needed to get some stuff for overnight. She hitched up her bag and marched ahead.

Within a few minutes, she'd got herself a toothbrush, some pants and a two pack of t-shirts big enough to sleep in. Katrin still hadn't called back.

She was standing by the side of the road, still debating whether to call Katrin again, when a taxi pulled up. Two girls, dressed in jeans, cold-shoulder tops and no coats got out. How did they not freeze to death?

Lara leapt in and grabbed the door before anyone else could get in. She slammed the door shut.

The cabbie, who was sorting out his money looked up. "Oh." He reset the meter. "Where to, love?"

"London?" she said, hopefully.

He laughed. When she didn't join in, he said, "Can't do that, love. Have you seen the weather?"

Given that she was damp, hungry and so cold she could barely feel her extremities, she wanted to cry. "I had noticed," she snapped.

The cabbie was unfazed. "So, unless you've got somewhere more realistic you want me to take you, I'm going to have to ask you to get out of my cab. I can do a couple more local trips before I knock off."

She found the location of the B and B on her phone and showed it to him. "Here. Can you take me here?"

He sucked his teeth. "Trewton Royd. I dunno, love. It's very steep out there. Not sure the car-"

The tears she'd been holding back, slid out of the corners of her eyes. "Please?" she said. "I'm hungry and I'm cold and I'm not dressed for the weather. There's nowhere to stay in this town and there seems to be a far right nationalists rally or something happening-"

"Oh. Hey. Don't cry." The cabbie turned round so that he could look at her. "I thought the rally had been cancelled, thank god."

"Yes, but so have the trains. There's a bunch of thugs wandering around, with nothing to do." She wiped her face with her sleeve and ended up even more damp than before.

The cabbie seemed to come to a decision. "Right then. I'll take you as close as I can to Trewton. If the snow starts settling, I might have to drop you off at the top of the hill. I might now be able to get back up the hill if it's slippery." He pulled cautiously out.

The relief made her cry even more. She sniffed and wiped her eyes. "Thank you."

"You're all right," he said. "My wife would never forgive me if I left a young girl to be harassed by Nazis."

Lara didn't respond. Ordinarily, she hated being called a girl. She was twenty nine, for heaven's sake. But his comment about Nazis hit home.

The car inched through traffic. "So," said the cabbie. "You Indian?"

Lara glanced at him. She couldn't tell much about him in the limited light, but he looked Asian. She weighed up her options. "Mum is," she said, quietly. "Dad's English."

He nodded, like that was exactly the answer he was expecting. "I'm from Pakistan. Well, not me, exactly. My folks are. I've never been."

She nodded, not wanting to get drawn into this conversation. She didn't want to trade stories of the second generation immigrant experience. "I'm starving. Is it okay if I eat in your cab?" she said.

"Not something eggy is it?" he said. "I can't stand egg or blue cheese. Anything else, you go for it."

She took a packet of crisps out of her bag. "It's crisps. Ready salted."

"You're fine, then."

By the time they got into the dark hillside, Lara knew more about Karim, the cab driver, than she'd ever wanted to know. On the other hand, he seemed quite a well-meaning man and his cab was dry and warm, so she just said 'hmm' and 'really' a lot and let him talk. He pulled to a stop at the top of the hill and sucked his teeth.

"Do you think it's too dangerous?" said Lara. She found her purse. She just wanted to get to this wretched pub and lie down. If she had to walk the last bit, she would. Anything to get this day to end.

"I can get you down, but I'm not sure I could get back up the hill again. It's looking quite icy, look."

Lara sighed. "Fine. How much do I owe you?"

He turned and looked at her. "I'm sorry, love. I feel really bad." He looked at the meter. "Call it a tenner and we'll leave it at that."

She glanced at the meter, which read £13.00. Was that all? Things were cheaper out here. "No. Just show me where to go." She handed him a twenty.

"I'll walk you there-"

"No. Go back. Get another fare," she said, thrusting the note at him. "So, where is it?"

He pointed down the hill, where the road ran through a small cluster of buildings. "The big one at the T junction. That's the pub. It's quite a steep hill. Do you have a torch?"

"I'll be fine," she said. "I have my phone." She waved away the proffered change, gathered her things and got out of the car. She popped her head back in to say thank you.

"You have a good Christmas," Karim said.

"You too."

He stayed there for a bit, letting her use the headlights to guide her. The hill was steep. She had to sling the handles of her bag over both shoulders, so that it rested like a really uncomfortable backpack, so that she had her hands free, in case she slipped. It was cold and the thin layer of snow had iced over. She could see what Karim meant.

Once the car left, she found herself in the dark, surrounded by velvet quiet night. Using the flashlight on her phone, she concentrated on getting one foot in front of the other until the ground levelled out and she was walking along an almost flat street.

Light spilled out from shops. Peering inside, she could see they were closing up. The pub windows glowed invitingly in the night. It looked warm. Warm would be so nice. She fixed her eyes on her destination and marched on.

By the time she stumbled into the pub, her teeth were chattering. The initial blast of heat as she walked into the main bar was almost painful, she was so cold. It took a few seconds for her eyes to adjust. The pub was, well ... pub-like. The place had a faded charm about it, with thick beams on the ceiling and brass fittings around the bar. They'd made an effort for Christmas, with tinsel and baubles hung up haphazardly over everything. A Christmas tree with flashing lights stood at the back, almost obscuring a quiz machine. There was a subtle smell of pine, probably from the Christmas tree.

A harassed looking man was moving boxes behind the bar. He looked up when she arrived.

"Hi," she said. "I'm-"

"Oh good, you're here," he said, smiling warmly. "My word, you look frozen. Come sit by the fire."

"Actually, I'd just like to check in and go to my room," she said. She stabbed at her phone, trying to bring up the booking email. Her hands were so cold, the phone didn't respond.

"Oh, no need to check in." He looked around. "Here, I'll take you up. Follow me." He led the way out and up some stairs. "I'm Phil, by the way," he said.

Lara made a noise in her throat.

"We've put you in our Tracey's old room," Phil continued. He took her along a landing, which had rooms leading off it and to a door without a number on it. "Here's your key to the family part," he said, handing her a key with a big tassel on it. He let her in and up more stairs. "We tend to lock the door behind us when we come up here," he said. "It's nice to keep things a bit separate, you know."

"Right." Looks like she got the last room in the place. It was up in the attic. From what he was saying, they'd given her a room that used to be in the private part of the inn. Her tired brain registered this, but she couldn't muster up the energy to ask questions. So long as she had a place to collapse, that was all she wanted.

"Here you are." He opened the door and ushered her into a tiny little bedroom with sloping ceilings. "There's an en suite," he said, pointing to what looked like a cupboard. "Just make yourself at home. Vinnie isn't here yet. If you come downstairs once you're sorted, we'll get you something to eat. How does that sound?"

"Sounds great. Thanks."

"I'd better get back. It's all a bit mad down there. I'll see you in a bit, love. It's lovely to meet you." He set off back down the stairs.

Lara closed the door to the tiny room and peeled off her damp coat. Poking her head into the 'en suite' she found that it was a tiny bathroom with a toilet and a shower cubicle. It was so small that the towel hook was on the door and there was barely room to turn around. Still, it was a shower. Oh god, she needed a shower.

She pulled stuff out of her bag and looked at the few things she had. When she'd left that morning, she had expected to be going home for the night, so she had no overnight things save what she'd bought just before catching the cab. She should have bought herself some leggings when she got the spare pants. Oh well, she'd just have to put her damp trousers back on. She put her phone in to charge, grabbed the towel that was on the bed and went to try out the shower. When she turned it on and found that it was hot, she nearly cried with relief.

Chapter 3

It was snowing in earnest by the time Tilly and Diane pulled into the pub car park. Tilly hauled her backpack out of the back and said goodbye.

"Think about what I said," Diane called, leaning out of the window.

"I will. Drive safely," Tilly called back. She hoisted up her back pack and made her way in.

There was a woman behind the bar. That must be Tracey's aunt Angie.

"Er… hi. I'm Thilini. Vinnie's sister." Tilly lowered her bag and leaned on the counter.

The woman beamed. "Oh hello, love! I'm Angie. Vinnie and Tracey aren't here yet. But we've got a room ready for you. Hang on a sec." She disappeared into a room in the back.

Tilly looked around at the bar. A few blokes were sitting at one end. They looked at her with mild curiosity. She grinned back at them. The both nodded to her, not unfriendly, but not exactly glowing with friendliness either.

"It's quiet," she observed, looking at the empty bar.

"It's early and the weather's bad," said one of the men.

"It'll liven up soon enough," the other added.

Angie returned. "I can't for the life of me find the key we set aside for you. Anyway, never mind. I'm sure it'll show up.

I'll show you to your room first though, so that you can drop your bags and freshen up. We've put you in Tracey's old room."

"Okay. Lead on."

Tilly followed Angie one set of stairs and then up the second, smaller set of stairs.

"Here we go," said Angie. "We tend to lock the door to this bit, because you never know with the guests... I will find you a key. In the meantime, just make yourself at home."

"Thank you so much," said Tilly. She opened the door and strode in.

At that same moment a door inside the room opened and woman stepped out wearing nothing but a towel. Both women screamed.

The other woman clutched the towel, which was wrapped around her, covering her breasts to her hips, but not much else. "What the hell??"

"Oh my god, I'm so sorry." Tilly backed out as fast as she could and shut the door. She turned to find Angie staring at the now closed door, looking aghast.

"It ... er... seems to be occupied," said Tilly. By an attractive woman, her hind brain supplied as it filed away the glimpse of slim shoulders and very nice legs. Brown skin, lighter than Tilly's but still brown.

Angie frowned. "You ARE Vinnie's sister, aren't you?" she said, her eyes narrow.

"I am. My name's Thilini. I've just got back from a year in Spain and I'm told I have the same eyes and eyebrows as him."

Angie scrutinised her. "So you do." She shook her head. "So, if you're Tilly... then who the bloody hell is that?" She pointed to the door.

Tilly shrugged. "No idea." She would quite like to find out who she was too. "And, er, what do we do?"

Angie seemed to come to a decision. "You leave your bag up here, and we'll go down to the bar and get you something to eat. I had a booking come in about an hour and a half ago. I have a nasty suspicion that Phil has done something very stupid. When I find him, I'm going to bloody kill him." She marched down the stairs.

O-kay. Tilly pushed her bag against the wall and ran after Angie.

The older woman locked the door when Tilly joined her on the landing and carried on down to the next floor, muttering under her breath. At the bottom of the stairs, she stopped, turned and put a hand on Tilly's arm. "I'm so sorry about this, love. We're usually much better than this."

"Um... I'm sure," Tilly said. What on earth was going on?

When they got into the bar, a man with short cropped grey hair was behind the bar.

"Phil," Angie snapped.

One of the guys at the bar nudged the other and said, "Ey up. Phil's in trouble."

"What's the matter, love?" Phil said. "I've been looking for you. Vinnie's sister's here."

"I know," said Angie. She walked behind the bar and folded her arms.

Tilly slid onto a bar stool to watch.

"This," Angie threw an arm out towards Tilly. "This is Vinnie's sister."

Tilly gave him a smile and little wave.

Phil's eyes went huge. He went pale. "Oh," he said. "Shit."

"And who have you put in the room we prepared for Tilly?" said Angie. "Hmm?"

"I'm ... I saw her come in and I was expecting Vinnie's sister, so I assumed..." He put his hand to his mouth. "Oh god. Oh, I'm so sorry," he said to Tilly.

"You saw a brown girl and assumed it was me," said Tilly, shaking her head and trying to keep a straight face. "That's some racist shit there, Phil."

Phil went bright red. "I ... I don't know what to say. I'm so sorry, love."

The men at the end of the bar started to laugh. "You've really done it this time, Phil."

"And you lot," Angie snapped at them. "You could've told me he'd already sent that poor girl up to Tilly's room."

The two regulars muttered 'sorry Ange' and looked at their pints.

Tilly smiled. "Don't worry about it," she said. "But if you could sort out somewhere for me to sleep, that'd be nice." She would have been angrier, but Vinnie really liked Phil and Angie. From what she knew, her brother was a good judge of character. If Vinnie said Phil was okay, then Phil was probably okay and it was quite likely to be just an awkward mistake.

"What are we going to do, Ange?" said Phil, turning to his wife. He looked horror struck.

Angie had gone into the office. Phil turned to follow her.

"Hey, Phil. At least get the lass a drink before you bugger off to be shot," one of the men said.

"Oh. Yes. Of course. What would you like, love? On the house."

"Ooh, he really must be feeling bad," said one of the jokers.

"I'll have a glass of red, please," Tilly said.

"House red okay?"

"House red is fine."

He poured her a big glass and passed it to her. "Here you go ... er... Te-lee-ni? Did I say that right?"

He hadn't. She considered correcting him and decided she couldn't be bothered. "Tilly. Just call me Tilly." She took the glass and smiled. "Thank you."

"Listen. I'm really sorry, okay." He looked over his shoulder.

Tilly shrugged. "You should be apologising to the other lady, not me. We walked in as she was coming out of the shower. I think we gave her quite a scare."

Phil groaned. "I've really messed up this time."

Angie came out of the office. "She must be the last minute booking that came through earlier. That's the only single room booking I've had that isn't a regular." She tapped a key, with a big wooden tag on it against her palm. "I can upgrade her to a double room ... and maybe dinner and a bottle of wine on the house ... but that's about all I can do. I suppose I'd better go and sort this out then." She glared at Phil, who looked suitably contrite. "Try not to screw anything else up in the meantime."

Chapter 4

Lara was still shaking by the time she finished getting dressed. Her trousers were damp, yuck, but at least the t-shirt was clean. It was too big, but she was beyond caring.

Fury bubbled in her chest. What kind of a place was this that let people randomly wander into rooms? The man said they kept the door to the stairs locked. Like hell they did. She looked at the key that she'd tossed on the small desk. He had given her a key to that door. She picked it up and let the tassels run through her fingers. For the first time, she looked at the room properly. It didn't look like a B and B room should. It was far too ... personal. There was a small collection of category romance novels on the shelf. An old boy band poster on the wall. Even the bedding looked faded and, she looked closely at it, was Harry Potter branded. Ravenclaw.

Weird.

A quick rummage in the desk revealed a hair dryer, a ruler and a random assortment of stationery. This definitely felt like someone's room, rather than a hotel. Lara dried her hair and was trying to use the hair dryer to warm up her trousers a bit so that they didn't feel so damp, when someone knocked on the door.

She put down the hair dryer and opened the door. At least this time they knocked.

An older woman stood outside. She smiled. "Hello. I'm Angie. I'm the landlady," she said. "I'm here to apologise for the mix up."

Lara took a step back into the room and said, "Go on, then. I wasn't expecting much, but I expected at least the luxury of privacy."

"I'm really sorry about that. We didn't know there was anyone in here." Angie gave a little sigh. "You see, we'd prepared this room for a private guest, family, if you like. My husband thought you were her and brought you up here. Then the real Tilly arrived and I didn't know you were here..."

Lara folded her arms. None of this was helping. She raised her eyebrows and glared at the older woman, waiting for a proper explanation.

"We have a room we'd prepared for you. If you don't mind, I can help you move your stuff... We've upgraded you to a double room and we'd like to offer you dinner, on the house. I'm really, really sorry about the mix up. I ... well, I've torn a strip off him, but it was genuinely a mistake."

"He didn't even ask my name."

"No. He was expecting you to be Tilly and when you came in looking all wet and cold, he thought he'd best get you settled right away. He's a twit sometimes, but his heart's in the right place."

Lara thought about the girl who had walked in. The one the man had mistaken her for. The girl had been tall, pretty and ... brown. "He mixed us up because we were both brown?"

Angie's frown deepened. "I suppose. But it might have happened if I'd said 'there's a red head coming, keep an eye out' and you'd been a redhead." She shook her head. "Anyway, the point is, I'm sorry. We'd like to offer you an upgraded room and dinner, if you'll accept it. With our profuse apologies."

Part of her felt she should make more of a fuss, but she was still hungry and dinner sounded great. A room with a lock on it sounded great too. She didn't have the energy left to fight. "Yes, fine," she said. "Apology accepted. Let me just get my stuff."

It took her barely a minute to gather her things and follow Angie.

The new room was much more like she'd expected. Neat and cosy, but with that impersonal feel that hotel rooms had. There was a folder next to the small kettle and tea making station. She flipped it open and found the Wi-Fi code. There was, she noticed, no actual phone signal. This place really was in the sticks. You had to rely entirely on the Wi-Fi. How did people survive out here before WhatsApp and Messenger?

Once the phone had linked up to the Wi-Fi, she threw her bag on the bed and went downstairs to the pub.

It was a bit livelier than before. A few more people were dotted about the place. Lara chose a table not far from the fire, a short distance from the bar. The man, Phil, rushed over and apologised some more. She could tell he was genuinely mortified, so she let him off. She ordered herself a lasagne and sat back. Since she hadn't eaten in a while, it was probably best not to drink too much, but she took a sip of wine and felt the warmth spread through her chest. The girl who had walked in on her was at the bar. She was talking to the two old guys sitting at the bar. Maybe she was local? She certainly seemed relaxed.

Lara took another sip of her wine and studied the girl, after all she'd seen more of Lara than was comfortable. She had long black hair, tied in a plait over one shoulder and was wearing a tunic over a pair of skinny jeans. Her features were sharp and pretty. She was attractive, Lara thought. Except there was something about her manner that set off alarms. The girl said something to the men and made an expansive hand gesture that made them laugh. There it was. Something in the tilt of the mouth and the twinkle in the eye that said 'mischief'.

One of the men replied and the girl laughed. It was a surprisingly deep laugh that suggested naughty things. Definitely trouble. She would have to stay away.

Lara sighed and looked down at her phone, half charged now. She'd been out with girls like that before. It never ended well.

She checked her emails, sent in notes on how her meeting had gone and dropped Kristin a line about the pub being warm and comfortable. She didn't mention the people walking in on her while she was half naked thing. Kristin didn't need to know that.

Her gaze inadvertently flicked towards the girl at the bar. She was looking at Lara. When they're glances caught, she smiled. Oh crap, she was coming over.

Aargh. Lara looked back at her phone. Try to look busy. The last thing she wanted was a conversation with someone who had seen her almost naked and wasn't actually a lover.

"Hi," the girl said.

"Uh... hi." Lara carefully put her phone down and looked up. Up close she could see that Tilly's tunic was actually a kameez worn over a long sleeved t-shirt. She had the clearest brown eyes. They sparkled. See? Mischief.

"Well, go on, then," said Lara.

"What?" Tilly's expression was all too innocent.

"You were about to say it was nice to see me with my clothes on, weren't you?"

For a second she looked like she was going to deny it, then she grinned. "Okay, you're right. I was. I'm predictable like that. Mind if I join you?"

Before Lara had chance to answer, she was already sitting down. "I'm Tilly." She held out her hand.

"Lara." They shook hands. Tilly's hands were warm and unexpectedly rough.

"So, what're you doing here, Lara?" said Tilly, picking up her own glass of red.

"Look, you don't have to come and chat with me. Just because we had that unfortunate run in."

"That is true. How about I come and chat with you because you clearly don't know anyone here. And neither do I. Also, we are the only two brown people in this room and that guy over there has been eyeing you up since the minute you sat down." She turned and smiled pointedly at a young man who was standing by the pool table further down the room. He looked surprised and turned away. Behind him his friend potted a ball.

Looking around, Lara realised that she was right. There were a few groups of people, families, knots of friends. All of them were white. The atmosphere wasn't unfriendly. She wished she hadn't noticed because now she was aware of it. It felt weird.

"And?" she said. "Maybe I do mind. Maybe I just want to be alone."

Tilly twitched an eyebrow at her. "In that case, that's fine. After the way we met, I feel … I should care about you."

"Right." Was she flirting with her? Did she mind? Lara hid her smile behind her glass. She didn't mind, really. It had been a while. "Okay," she said. "I'll play. Let's see ... I'm Lara, as I said. I was at a business meeting in Huddersfield and all the trains were cancelled and I couldn't get home. This was the nearest available guest house. How about you?"

"I'm meeting my- oh." She stopped talking as Phil appeared holding a tray containing two plates.

"Here we are," he said. "Lasagne for you." He put Lara's plate in front of her. "And burger with chips for you." He popped Tilly's plate down. "Sorry about the wait, love. I thought you might like to eat together."

"Phil, just because we're both brown doesn't mean we're friends," said Tilly.

Phil went red. "I ..."

"I'm joking, Phil. I'm joking."

"It's fine," said Lara, giving Tilly a warning glare. It wasn't nice to tease the poor man. He had screwed up, but clearly, it bothered him that he had. "Thank you" she said to Phil. "This looks delicious."

"Can I get you anything else?"

"No. This is fine," said Lara. When Phil left, she said, "So, you're joining me then? Whether I want company or not. Are you always this pushy?"

"Are you always this rude?" Tilly picked up the burger and turned it, as though trying to find an entry point.

Was she being rude? Yes, she was. "Look," she said. "I've had the worst day. I'm wearing damp jeans, my hair is a frizzy mess and I'm starving. I'm sorry if I was rude. It's just been ... a bit much. Okay."

Tilly's gaze softened. "I'm sorry too. You're right. If you want a bit of privacy, you should have it. I'll leave you in peace." She started to gather up her plate and cutlery. Lara felt guilty. Also, she suddenly realised that she didn't really want to sit there by herself. Not now.

"No, please. Stay," she said.

Tilly looked up at her, half standing. "Sure?"

"Yes. It'll be nice to have … some company."

Tilly settled back down. "I promise not be so full on. I know I can be a bit much. Especially when I'm nervous."

Lara took a mouthful of lasagne and closed her eyes momentarily with pleasure. She hadn't realised she was so hungry. She savoured it. Across the table from her, Tilly bit into her burger.

"You're nervous?" Lara said, after a few minutes. "Why?"

"Oh, you know. Christmas. Family. I've been away for the last couple of Christmases. I decided to come back this time at kinda short notice... so my parents have gone off on holiday... and my friends are all spending their holidays with their folks … so I'm here."

"Your family don't do Christmas, then?"

"Nah. We're Buddhist. Well, my mum is." Tilly put the burger down and dabbed some mayonnaise off the side of her mouth. The door to the bar opened, bringing a gust of cold and Tilly turned to look. She turned back. "I'm either an atheist or agnostic or something."

"Which?"

"I guess if I'm not sure, agnostic." Tilly grinned. "I don't really worry about it, to be honest. You?"

"I was brought up Catholic. Mum was pretty devout." Lara loaded up her fork with exaggerated care. She remembered going to church, clutching her mother's hand. After her mother died, she and her father had carried on going to church, until her father met her step mother. After that Lara had stopped going. Church was her mother's place. She couldn't bear to see her stepmother in it, her blonde head leaning towards dad in the same way her mother's dark head had done.

"Hopefully, the weather will improve so that you can get home to them for Christmas." Tilly said. She took a big bite of her burger and made an appreciative noise.

"Hmm." Lara wasn't intending to go home for Christmas. Why would she? Her father and his wife had a new family now. She wasn't really part of it. Christmas to her, was a nice relaxing day in her flat. With good food and good telly. Why would anyone want more?

"Does that mean you don't think the weather will improve?"

Lara looked up to find Tilly looking at her shrewdly. Damn. This woman was actually paying attention. "Erm... no. I mean I'm not going to my family for Christmas. I tend to spend Christmas day at home. By myself."

Tilly gave it a few minutes' thought. "I guess that could be quite nice. A day off without family." She gave a little snort. "I love my family, but they are maddening."

"My family don't really know what to do with me," Lara said, without thinking about it. Crap. She shouldn't have said that. Now she'll have to explain. She hated explaining.

Tilly gave her a questioning look and popped a chip in her mouth.

Lara sighed. "My ... mother died a few years ago. Dad remarried. They have a small child. It's awkward."

"I'm sorry," Tilly said. She sounded genuinely sad. Thankfully, she didn't try to dig any further. "Must be nice to have a little brother or sister," she said. "I bet they think you're amazing."

Lara thought of the soft little bundle her stepmother had handed to her. The plump face that looked weirdly familiar. Those tiny little pink fists. She wasn't a natural with babies and she'd been glad her half-brother had been asleep. She hadn't seen him since. He'd be one now. Did he think she was amazing? "I doubt it," she said. "I've only met him once."

When Tilly didn't say anything, Lara filled the silence with, "He's only my half-brother anyway. Dad's a completely different person now. It's not like we've got anything in common."

Tilly said, "That sounds... hard. Families are complicated." She returned to her food.

Lara waited for the lecture about family and love and whatever. People always seemed to want to tell her about the importance of family, like she'd never thought about it herself. She and her dad messaged each other. He What'sApped her pictures of baby Henry. She told him about any advances at work. There was really not a lot else to discuss. It worked for them. She didn't understand why people couldn't accept that.

But there was no lecture. The door to the bar opened and Tilly turned in her seat to see who it was, before turning back. "I have two big brothers," she said. "They drive me mad. They're quite a bit older than me. Super high achievers. Both lawyers, you know. I'm the loser in the family."

"What do you do?"

"I'm an artist and sculptor." She caught Lara's gaze and held it, as though challenging her to find fault with that.

"That's interesting." She was genuinely interested. She didn't often meet people who worked in the arts. "Does it pay well?"

Tilly's eyes narrowed momentarily, then her expression cleared and she laughed. "No. Of course not. It's art!" She shook her head and looked down at her plate. "But it does travel well. I've just spent a year in Spain, working in a studio of a fairly big artist. The pay was shit, but it's improved my Spanish no end."

"It is someone famous?"

Tilly named an artist Lara had never heard of.

"So no, not famous here, but well known enough in Spain to be given a large public commission."

"Right. So, what's next then? Are you going to carry on working for him?"

It seemed that was the wrong question to ask. Tilly's expression clouded over. She took another bite of her burger and avoided Lara's eye. Okay. Clearly, she wasn't the only one with issues. Lara returned to her meal. It was delicious. She couldn't tell whether it was the fact that she was so tired and hungry that made it so. Or perhaps it was the company. She sneaked a glance at Tilly, who was currently licking ketchup off her thumb. She was cute. Pretty, in a sharp featured way, but more than that it was that gleam in her eye, that sense of mischief that intrigued Lara. It was something she didn't see often. She knew it meant trouble, but she couldn't help herself.

She wondered whether Tilly had been romantically involved with the artist guy in Spain. Was that why she'd been upset when going back was mentioned? Not that she cared, really. It had nothing to do with her. Lara reminded herself that she was talking to Tilly because she didn't know anyone here and Tilly was the friendliest face there was at this moment.

"This is excellent," she said, gesturing to her plate.

"So's this," said Tilly. "I'm told, they use meat from local farms where they can, so that could be what makes the difference. Also, I gather Angie is a pretty good cook." She picked up a chip. "I'm really looking forward to Christmas dinner, if this is the case."

Before Lara could think of a response, the door opened again and a tall man in a greatcoat came in. Tilly gave a little squeak, threw down her chip and bolted off. She threw her arms around the man, who picked her up in hug.

Lara felt a stab of emotion. Anger? Jealousy? She looked down at her meal. Why did she feel that? Why did she feel anything at all about who Tilly was hugging? Her gaze dragged itself back to Tilly, just in time to see the man place a kiss on the top of her head. A woman, also bundled up in a coat, who had followed him in, smiled at them both and disappeared behind the bar to greet Angie. Ah. Angie had referred to Tilly as someone's sister. That must be the brother then.

The wash of relief she felt worried her even more than the initial stab of jealousy did.

TILLY GAVE HER BROTHER a tight squeeze and released him so that she could get a good look at him. "You look ... good, actually. You look really well." What she wanted to say was that he looked happy, but that seemed too obvious a thing to say.

Vinnie grinned at her. "You look good too. I can tell Amma you look like you're eating properly."

Tilly rolled her eyes. "I TOLD her, but she never believes me."

Vinnie's girlfriend reappeared. She had straight black hair with a single stripe of green in it and thick rimmed glasses.

Vinnie put an arm around her as she came to stand next to him. "Tilly, this is Tracey. Tracey, this is my baby sister, Thilini."

"Hi Tilly," Tracey smiled at her.

Tilly leaned in and gave her a quick kiss on the cheek. "I've heard so much about you," she said. "From Vinnie and from Mum. All of it good, which is pretty impressive."

"Likewise," said Tracey.

Tilly snorted. "I bet Mum said some choice things about me."

"Actually, she's quite proud of you."

She didn't believe that for a minute. But least said, soonest mended. "Was your trip awful?"

"Not great," said Vinnie. He took off his glasses and rubbed his eyes. "I could do with some dinner and a pint."

"I've got the key to our room," said Tracey. She turned to Tilly. "Would you mind if we just went up and dropped our bags?"

"Oh sure," said Tilly. "I'm having my dinner anyway." She nodded to where Lara was sitting. "I'm over there, sitting with ... Lara. "

Vinnie put his glasses back on and raised his eyebrows. "That's fast work. You've only been here ten minutes and you've pulled already."

"Shhh." Tilly felt the heat rise in her cheeks. "Vinnie!"

"Oh." Vinnie dropped his voice. "I was joking, but wow. Have you pulled already?" He glanced at Lara. "She seems nice."

"I haven't pulled. We're just getting to know each other, that's all." Tilly whispered back. "She is nice. But she's really cranky. She's had a really bad day." And she was so pretty. So, very pretty.

"Ah, okay. Well, we'll let you get back to talking to her, then." Vinnie turned to follow Tracey out of the room. "Good luck."

"Thanks."

Tilly went and sat back at the table. "That was my brother, Vinnie," she informed Lara, who shrugged.

They both continued their meals in silence. Lara finished and put down her cutlery with a satisfied sigh.

Tilly dipped another chip in the ketchup and sneaked a glance at Lara. She looked a lot happier now. She wasn't sure what it was about her that pulled her in. She fancied the really nice legs and that graceful sweep of her neck and shoulders, obviously. But apart from that, there was something fragile about Lara. As though, hidden under the prickly exterior, there was someone sad and in need of a cuddle. Tilly knew she was a sucker for that. If only she could get Lara to hang around for a bit, she might get her to unbend a little.

"So, what're you going to do now," she said. "Want another glass of wine?"

Lara didn't meet her eye. "I might just turn in, to be honest. I'm exhausted."

Oh no. She'd been hoping to get to know this woman a little better. "But it's only just gone seven."

Lara looked genuinely surprised. She checked her phone. "Oh, so it is. I ... thought it was much later."

"So, can I get you another drink?"

Lara looked up at her, a crease on her forehead. Tilly tried not to look too keen.

"No," said Lara, slowly. "I think I'm going to go to bed. I genuinely am exhausted."

"Oh. Okay. I might see you tomorrow then."

"I'll be off first thing."

Goodness, this girl was hard work. Tilly gave up. "I see. Well, enjoy your new room."

Lara rolled her eyes. "At least this one has a proper lock," she said. She stood up. "It was nice to meet you Tilly. Have a great Christmas."

"You too." Tilly watched as Lara went over to the bar and spoke to Phil, before heading out. At the door, Lara paused and looked back. When Tilly grinned at her, she flushed and turned away.

Tilly turned back to her drink and settled down more comfortably in her seat. Oh well. You couldn't blame a girl for trying.

Chapter 5

Tilly was having breakfast with Vinnie and Tracey. At the moment, she was busy polishing off her breakfast bacon sandwich.

"You're right," she said as she dabbed the corner of her mouth. "That is a very nice bacon sandwich."

"Told you," said Vinnie, who had just finished his own.

Tracey rolled her eyes. "You emailed her to tell her about the bacon sandwiches? You are so weird."

"And the cinnamon buns. I got a very long message about cinnamon buns," Tilly added.

"I despair," said Tracey. She reached for the teapot and bumped her hand against the milk. Vinnie stayed her hand. "Let me," he said. He picked up the teapot and replenished both her cup and his.

"You've trained him to pour your tea?" Tilly looked at Tracey with new appreciation.

"Ha," said Vinnie. "I've learned the hard way not to let Tracey pour hot things anywhere near me."

"I have problems with depth perception," Tracey told Tilly. "But I can pour a cup of tea without disaster, thanks."

"Remember what happened last time?" said Vinnie.

"Oh, that wasn't an accident," said Tracey darkly. But her expression took any sting out of her words.

Tilly watched her brother laugh. She hadn't seen him this happy in ages. Amma was right. He and Tracey were well suited. That was nice. Vinnie was built for being settled and boring. Not that Tracey was boring. It must be fun being with a tech millionaire.

"So, what's the plan for today, then?" she said.

"It's the pub Christmas party this evening," said Tracey. "I was planning on helping Aunty Angie with whatever she needed doing."

Vinnie shrugged. "I'm up for that." He looked fondly at his girlfriend. "Last year's party was something special."

"Oh yeah. That's when you guys got together, right?" Tilly had heard all about it. She had spent Christmas in a drunken haze in a friend's house. She remembered talking to her mother a few days later and being relieved to hear that for once, Amma was too busy worrying about Vinnie being snowbound in a remote village to berate Tilly about how she'd messed up her life. "I can help with the decorations ... or anything really." She wiggled her fingers. "I'm pretty good with my hands."

"Oh yeah. How did the art installation turn out in the end? Is it open now?" Vinnie asked.

"Not yet. The opening is in January. Jorge is going to do the fine details in the next few weeks." She braced herself for what was coming next.

"So what are you going to do afterwards?" said Vinnie. "Go back to Spain? Find a new contract?"

Tracey looked from one to the other. "I'm ... just going to take the plates into the kitchen." She gathered up the empty breakfast plates.

"You can't leave me with him when he's about to go into big brother mode," said Tilly.

"Oh, I think I can," said Tracey, smiling. "Watch." She walked off, holding the plates carefully in both hands.

Tilly sighed.

"Really though, Tilly," Vinnie said. "What are your plans? Why don't you get something in the UK for a change? If you don't want to be too close to home, there's a thriving arts scene in Leeds."

"I don't want to move to Leeds, Vin."

"You don't have to. But you do need to think about your future and settle down somewhere. You want to be an artist, that's great, but you need to make money somehow. I'm happy to bail you out every so often, but I can't keep doing it. That would just be enabling you in your weird nomadic lifestyle."

"But I don't do settling down. I don't do commitment. You know that."

Vinnie sighed and pinched the bridge of his nose. "But why not? What are you afraid of?"

Tilly stared at him, unable to articulate what she felt. She looked up, searching for a distraction.

"WHAT DO YOU MEAN, THERE are still no trains running? It's been nearly 24 hours!" Lara paced the room, mobile phone clapped to her ear. With no phone reception, she was doing everything by VOIP calls. Thank goodness this place had Wi-Fi.

"It's only been twelve hours," said Kirstin. "And the next available train is at 1pm ... possibly."

"Well, let's get that one, then."

"I dunno," said Kristin. "I can't book you on. And the train is subject to confirmation, so ... it might not run at all. You might turn up and find that it's not running after all."

Lara chewed on her lip.

"And even if it did run," Kirsten continued. "It would be rammed full of impatient people. Look, why don't you just take this as a sign and take a couple of days off? We're shut from mid-afternoon onwards anyway, so it's not like you'll be coming into work."

"I can't do that," Lara snapped.

"Why not? No one's going to be buying logistics software between Christmas Eve and the twenty seventh, are they? Is the B&B comfortable?"

"Um. Yes, yes it's fine," Lara replied.

"Well there you are then. Just stay a couple of days. Relax, take in the scenery or something."

"I need clothes."

"Buy some? Aren't there shops Yorkshire?" Kirsten's voice was getting taut.

"I have to get home."

"What for?" said Kirsten. "What's waiting for you here?"

Lara stopped pacing. What was waiting for her there? Her own bed, a couple of Gŭ puddings in the fridge ... and that was it. There wasn't a girlfriend or group of friends waiting for her return. She didn't even have a cat. But it wasn't Kirsten's place to point this out. "Just do your job and get me back."

There was a second of silence. Then Kirsten said, "I can't. I can't buy you a ticket, because the website isn't selling any. You're somewhere warm and safe. If you want to go out and spend Christmas Eve travelling in shit weather and shit traffic, you can, but you don't get to speak to me like that. Merry bloody Christmas to you Lara." There was a click and she hung up.

"Kirsten-" Oh crap. She hadn't meant to be so rude. She rang back. It rang for a bit and a male voice answered. Martin, one of the security guards from the building staff. Although they weren't linked to the Haulistic Solutions, the security guys liked to pop in from time to time. Not least because Kirsten kept a box of biscuit assortments in her desk drawer.

"Hi Martin. It's me, Lara."

"Oh hey, Lara. What did you say to Kirsten? She's in a right snit."

"I ... ah... I was quite rude to her. Please can you tell her I'm sorry. I'll call again in a bit. I didn't mean to snap, it's just..."

"Oh, she'll come round," he said. "She always does."

Kirsten must have been upset if she abandoned the phone to Martin. For all her abruptness, Kirsten was meticulous in her duties. Toby joked that she took the phone with her even when she went to the loo.

Once Lara hung up, she reflected that yes, Kirsten did always come round. She and Kirsten got into these rows a lot. Was that because Kirsten was particularly sensitive? For the first time, she wondered if it was because she herself was unusually blunt. Who could she ask?

She glanced at the clock. Her stomach rumbled. There was still time to get breakfast. Tilly might be downstairs though.

She'd had a weirdly explicit dream about Tilly the night before. The dream was easily explained by the whole embarrassment factor of being walked in on ... but it still bothered her.

She checked her reflection in the mirror, pulled her hair back into a ponytail and added a swipe of lip gloss by way of looking presentable. She had to wear yesterday's clothes, but that would have to suffice. Pulling her clothes straight, she told herself to get a grip. Okay, so she found Tilly attractive. A bit. No one needed to know that. She could be cool and detached. Cool and detached was practically her calling card.

Lara was still telling herself this when she went into the bar downstairs. Tables had been set out with breakfast menus propped up. A few groups of people were sitting together, munching toast and reading newspapers.

"Lara."

Oh. There Tilly was, sitting with her brother. She waved and beckoned Lara over.

Lara hesitated. Did she really want to sit with Tilly? After all, she had inadvertently revealed too much about herself, in more ways than one, to this girl she hardly knew. Besides, what was the point of making friends when she was only here for another day at most? For a second the words 'holiday fling' waltzed tantalisingly through her head, but she dismissed the thought as soon as she registered it. She couldn't presume.

Tilly waved again. People were starting to look. Since she was stuck here, she may as well make an effort to be friendly.

"Morning," said Tilly, as Lara came near. "Sleep okay?"

She couldn't possibly know. Lara felt her face heating up, regardless. "Um. Yes. Thank you."

"Lara, this is my brother Vinnie. Vinnie. Lara."

Vinnie gave Tilly a meaningful look before he looked up and said, "Pleased to meet you, Lara."

They made small talk until someone came to take Lara's breakfast order. She chose to have porridge, despite Vinnie's enthusiastic recommendation of the bacon sandwich.

"So, are you stuck here for Christmas, then?" Tilly said.

"Looks like it. Are any of the shops open today? I could do with a change of clothes." She gestured to her work suit.

"We can ask Tracey," said Tilly, as the other woman returned to her seat. "Tracey - Lara needs to buy some clothes. What shops are there in the village?"

"Oh. Er... nothing that does clothes. You might be able to buy a jumper from the art shop, they sometimes have hand knitted things," said Tracey. "Otherwise, there's the charity shop and that's about it." She gave Lara and assessing glance. "We could probably find you a jumper and a few bits, if you like. We have a stash of things that guests left behind or, basically things that used to be mine."

"Yes, please." It didn't hurt.

"Oh, Tracey, Lara's in the tech sector too." Tilly turned to Tracey and beamed.

Oh dear. 'Tech' meant different things to different people. With men, it could mean anything from being the CEO of Oracle to being a shop assistant at PC World. Tilly being an artsy type, heaven knows what she classed as 'working in the tech sector'.

"Okay," said Tracey, looking surprised. "Er... What do you do, Lara?"

"I work for a company that sells software based logistics solutions for haulage firms," she said.

Tracey's eyebrows shot up. "What's your company called?"

"Haulistic Solutions."

"Oh." Tracey clicked her fingers. "You're a spinout for Liverpool Uni, right? I read about your work."

"Yes. I was the Masters student working on the logistics side. I was employee number two. My friend Toby was the software guy. He was employee number one." It was so nice to have someone remember where the work had come from. Her research and Toby's coding skills based on a method devised by their old boss, who was still a major shareholder. It was unusual for someone to know that detail though. "What do you do?"

"I'm ... uh..." Tracey gave Vinnie a glance. He made encouraging motions with his hands. "I used to be a tech entrepreneur. We used to have a start-up called Nifty Gift it. We sold up a little over a year ago."

Suddenly the familiarity fell into place. "Oh my god! You're Tracey Grahams!" How could she have failed to recognise her? "You and Giselle Lloyd really inspired me when I was starting out. It's such a male dominated world and you were there kicking arse and taking names. Oh wow. I can't believe I've met you. Here in-" She stopped. Tilly was making little shaking motions with her head. "Er ... here in a pub," she finished, weakling.

Tracey laughed. "It's my aunt's pub," she said. "But you can call it the middle of nowhere, if you want to. This is my home, if you like."

"What are you doing now? Are you working on something else?" Lara was suddenly aware that she was talking really fast. "I mean, if you're allowed to say."

"I'm not, actually, allowed to say," said Tracey, beaming. "I am working on something new though."

They chatted a little more, Lara trying really hard not to fangirl and failing. Beside her, Tilly and Vinnie were in some sort of earnest sotto voce discussion. Talking to Tracey was an education. Lara had read a lot about Tracey over the years and meeting one of her heroines in such an unexpected way made up for all the inconvenience of the night before. What was more, Tracey seemed to rate Haulistics as a good product. Just wait till she told Toby!

They were interrupted by Angie bustling past and saying, "If you're planning to help, we should get started."

"Oh. Yes, of course." Tilly was on her feet in seconds. "I'm pretty good with decorations. Shall I take care of those?"

"I'm just going to go find Lara some clothes from the spares box," said Tracey. "Poor thing's stuck here with just what she's got on." She turned and beckoned to Lara. "Come with me." As an afterthought, she said, "Can I go rummage in the room you're staying in, Tilly?"

"Go ahead." Tilly grinned. "See you in a bit, Lara."

The boxes under Tilly's bed yielded a couple of chunky jumpers, a few old coding conference t-shirts and a pair of paint flecked overalls.

"If you want," said Tracey. "I can ask Auntie Angie to bung your things through the wash."

"Oh, I don't want to add to her work. I'll change into these and come join you downstairs."

The overalls were far too big. Judging by the rolled up trouser legs they had been too big for Tracey too. Wishing she had bought a full change of clothes in Huddersfield the night before, Lara got changed. She looked ridiculous dressed in overalls, a jumper and her work pumps, but at least she was clean.

By the time she got downstairs, the others had started work. Tilly was standing on a chair, hanging up fake evergreen garlands. She turned when Lara walked in. Her gaze moved down and up.

Lara flushed. She looked terrible. Even though she didn't WANT to care about what Tilly thought, she couldn't help herself. Since she couldn't run away now, she chose to be icy.

"Yes," she said. "I know it's ridiculous. But I'm not awash with choices."

"Those were huge on me too," said Tracey, appearing with a box full of baubles.

"I think it's cute," said Tilly. She stepped carefully off the table onto a chair. "Okay Vinnie, turn them on."

Apparently the fake greenery had tiny LEDs embedded in it. Points of light glowed from inside the deep green. Tilly jumped onto the ground and started at it, with her hands on her hips. "Have we got anything we can add to that to lift it a bit," she said, frowning. "Something with a bit of sparkle."

"Tinsel and baubles," said Tracey.

"Hmm." Tilly came and stood next to Lara at the entrance to the bar. "Where do you want people to go to first? The bar? Or the food?"

"Bar," Phil called out from behind said bar.

"In that case, we should move the Christmas tree to over there," said Tilly. "Draws the eye and they end up pretty much at the bar."

Lara looked across. The Christmas tree was currently nicely out of the way, hiding the quiz machine behind it.

Within minutes, Tilly was running the decorating. When she made any changes to the existing decorations, she explained why. Lara joined Vinnie and Tracey in pinning, looping and hanging things to Tilly's specifications. While they worked, the siblings teased and joked with each other. Every so often Tracey would join in. At one point, Lara made a sarcastic comeback to which Tracey said, "I'd high five you for that, but I might accidentally smack you in the face."

Lara felt a glow of happiness. She was friends with Tracey Grahams. Who would have thought!

As it neared lunchtime, punters drifted in. A few stopped to comment on how good the pub looked.

"We've had the professional artists in this year," Angie said, and Lara felt proud on Tilly's behalf.

When they finally sat down for lunch, Lara got the chance to look at their handiwork. Moving the Christmas tree made the quiz machine a bit more obvious. Its new position drew people to the bar, but it also divided the room up a little so that the space beyond the bar felt cosier.

The pub was picturesque in a quaint old-fashioned sort of way. Where before the decorations had looked haphazard and tired, Tilly's rearrangement of the furniture and decorations had made it look tasteful and divided the space into semi enclosed spaces, with a clear route to flow between them. Less, it seemed, really was more. Overall, it looked cosy, inviting and Christmassy.

More to the point, she had enjoyed the relaxed atmosphere of working in a small group. When she'd finally lowered her guard long enough to laugh and allow Tilly to gently tease her without being defensive, she had actually enjoyed herself. The atmosphere reminded her a little of the early days at Haulistic Solutions when they'd been a tiny team of two, working together to get the service out of the door. She had forgotten how that used to be. When had it stopped being fun and become a chore? She thought about how she had snapped at Kirsten. She hadn't been like that at the beginning. When had she become such a humourless bitch?

Chapter 6

"**B**limey, this hill is steep," Lara puffed as they trudged up the incline that led out of the village.

"You're not wrong." Tilly stopped and put her hands on her knees. "I think I'm getting a stitch."

Lara stopped walking and leaned against the snow dusted stone wall. Tilly joined her, still holding her side.

"How wedded are you to the idea of getting a phone signal?"

Lara put her hand against the reassuring weight of her phone in the pocket of the hideous overalls. "I dunno."

"I mean, are you actually expecting anyone to have called you the old fashioned way? Wouldn't they have just WhatsApped or emailed instead?"

"I suppose." Lara pulled out the phone and checked for a signal. Nothing. Looking up the hill, it looked huge. Coming down it, carrying her laptop bag, in the dark had been bad enough. Did she really need to trudge up the bloody thing again? What if no one had phoned? It would have been all for nothing. Her legs really hurt. "Oh fine," she said. "We should go back."

"Thank god," said Tilly, resting her head back against the wall.

"I thought you didn't believe in god."

"I'd believe in anything that gives me a break from climbing this hill," Tilly said.

Lara laughed. "All right then, let's go back."

"I bloody love you."

Lara looked sharply across at Tilly, but the other woman was already setting off. She hadn't meant it. It was just a joke; a throwaway comment. Phew. That was good ... she didn't want to get into anything right now. So why did she feel this sense of disappointment?

Tilly turned and looked over her shoulder. "You coming, then?"

They started walking back down the hill, taking care not to slip. Thankfully, Tracey had found Lara a pair of wellies that fit. Doing this walk in her work shoes was asking for injury.

The snow from the night before had hardened into crunchy frost. Everything was edged in white. The sky was clearer today and it didn't look like more snow was due. It was so cold that Lara could feel the rawness in her eyes and nostrils.

"You didn't have to come with me in the first place, you know," she said to Tilly.

"I know, but I didn't want you to walk out here alone. Besides, just look at this view." She swept her arm out to indicate the white dusted hills, cut into squares by dark lines of dry stone walling. Nothing moved apart from puffs of cloud drifting across the ice blue sky. Tilly took a deep breath. "I'd forgotten how beautiful it was around here."

Lara looked too, not at the landscape, but at Tilly, with her face bright from exertion and her hair escaping from the woolly hat she'd rammed on her head, Tilly looked a picture of health and happiness. She glowed. When she turned to look back up the road they'd walked down, Lara could examine the lines of her features. So very pretty.

"Just look at those cottages," Tilly said.

Lara looked. A row of four cottages huddled together at the top of the hill. "What about them?"

"The way they're set against the bleakness of the moorland behind them. Just imagine what this place must look like in the summer."

"Maybe you should come back in the summer to see," Lara said.

Tilly turned. Her expression closed in. "We should get back." She started to walk again.

Puzzled, Lara followed. "What?" she said. "Did I say something wrong?"

"No, it's not you," said Tilly. "It's me. I ... don't go back to places. I rarely stop anywhere very long, to be honest."

"Why not?"

Tilly shrugged. "That's just how I am. I move. I travel. I experience the .... width of life, rather than the depth."

Lara gave that some consideration. "That doesn't make sense," she said. "I get the bit about wanting to see life, but why does that mean you can't come back? Surely, if you find the thing you're looking for-"

Tilly made a noise in her throat. "I'm not LOOKING for anything."

"In that case, what are you running away from?"

Tilly stopped and glared at her. "Not you too. Has Vinnie put you up to this?"

"Vinnie? What? No. What are you talking about?" The sudden change alarmed Lara. "Tilly?"

But Tilly seemed to be looking through her.

"Tilly." Worried now, Lara put her hand on the other woman's arm.

Tilly's attention seemed to come back to the present. "Sorry," she said. "No. Of course Vinnie didn't set you up to it. I'm sorry." She smiled. And just like that, she was back. "So, where do you want to explore next?"

"What was-"

But Tilly had already set off again. "Come on."

The road went down the hill and levelled off a little before the pub. The pub was at a T-junction where the road bent off to the left and led to a row of shops. They went to investigate. On one side of the road was a largish restaurant, which appeared to be busy. On the other side was a corner shop that Lara had noticed before and a selection of small shops. They were all closed.

They carried on walking on the road that went past the pub. It climbed a little way, with the church at the crest of the hill. Behind it, the Pennine hills towered in the background. Tilly stopped walking and gawped. "Wow." She took out her mobile phone and started to take a video.

Even without an artist's eye, Lara could see it was a beautiful spot. The sun had come out and in the sharp winter sunshine, everything stood out in high definition. It was so beautiful it was almost an assault on the senses. The frost rimed trees, the gleam of ice giving texture to the dark stone, the absolute clarity of the hills... it all made Lara feel breathless. Then she heard singing.

For a second, she was a little girl again, holding onto her mother's hand, standing outside the church in Croydon. The air smelled faintly of cars and of the spicy pomander they had been making at home. And people were singing the same carol.

Lara raised her hand to her chest and turned towards the church. There were no cars and no pomander, but the singing was still there.

Tilly said, "Are you okay?"

"Carols," said Lara.

"It's the children's service," said Tilly. "Look, it says so on the notice board."

"Ah." Lara felt like she was in a dream. "Okay."

"Would you ... like to go in?" said Tilly.

Lara looked at her, suddenly aware that she did, very much, want to go in. "Would you mind?"

"Of course not, daftie." Tilly linked arms with her. "I'm sure I can go into a church without bursting into flames."

They marched up the little path, past snow dusted graves, to the church door. They slipped inside and stood at the back. The hymn came to an end and everyone sat down. Lara sank into a pew at the back, with Tilly next to her.

The priest gave a short sermon, but Lara barely heard it. She revelled in the feeling of familiarity. The chill in the air, the rustling of people and prayer books. The echoey voice of the priest. It was all so familiar. It all reminded her of her mother. All that was different about this church was the smell. There wasn't the hint of incense here.

The congregation stood for another hymn. Tilly thrust a book, open to the right page, under her nose, but Lara found she already knew the words, some of them, anyway. She stood, shoulder to shoulder with her new friend and raised her voice, loud and strong, like her mother taught her. Caught in the moment, she felt almost at peace.

They sang another hymn. After that, they sat down for a moment of prayer and contemplation.

The moment she bowed her head, she felt her mother's absence. She'd been to grief counselling. She knew this happened, but the sense of loss hadn't been so strong for a long time. Her mother was gone. Her father had a new family. Even if he still kept in touch, he couldn't deal with the 'wrongness' of her sexuality. His comment when she told him had been 'thank goodness your mother wasn't here to hear this'. Was he right? Would Mama have hated her because she liked girls rather than boys? She'd never know. Her mama had taught her to be herself, so that was what she was doing. Studying business, rather than science like her father wanted, and now running a small business with her colleague. Sure, she wasn't rolling in money, but she was being herself as hard as she could. But it would be so nice if someone else appreciated it. To have someone say 'I see how hard you're working. I'm proud of you'. But there was no one.

Lara's jaw clenched and her whole body shivered. Tears leaked from under her eyelids. She was so very alone.

A warm hand wrapped itself around hers. Lara opened her eyes to see Tilly peering anxiously at her. She wasn't alone. Tilly was here.

Tilly mouthed 'shall we go?'

Lara nodded. She didn't want to draw attention to herself, so she squeezed Tilly's hand and waited until the priest spoke again. Tears still running down her face, she listened as he led them in the Lord's Prayer. When the service ended, they stood up and left the church before anyone could talk to them.

Lara rushed straight up to her room, slammed the door behind her and sank down onto her bed. The tears were still coming. Someone knocked on the door. It must be Tilly. Lara said 'come in'.

Tilly looked worried. She quietly shut the door before coming over to sit beside Lara. "What happened?" she asked. She passed a box of tissues from the bedside cupboard across.

Lara took a tissue and shook her head. "Don't know." A sob caught in her throat.

"Would you like a hug?" Tilly said, opening her arms.

Lara nodded. She laid her head against Tilly's shoulder and cried. Tilly stroked her hair and whispered kind things. After a few minutes, the tears subsided, but Lara remained where she was, with her head on Tilly's shoulder and her arms loosely around the other woman's waist. It was so nice to be held. It had been so long since someone had just held her.

Tilly smelled nice. Some sort of floral perfume mingled with citrus shampoo. And she was so warm and soft. When had she last slept with someone? Not since before the company started. A little voice piped up that this was the wrong time for this. Tilly was lovely and friendly and all that, but ... flirting was complicated. Relationships were complicated. But right now, she needed this contact. Was that so wrong?

"Want to talk about it?" Tilly said.

For a second, she thought Tilly had heard her thoughts, then realised she meant the crying. Lara reluctantly drew away and wiped her eyes. "I'm sorry about that," she said. "I'm not sure what came over me."

Tilly tilted her head to the side and said nothing.

"I... haven't been to church in a long time," Lara said. "I used to go with my mum."

"Ah," said Tilly, quietly. "I see. Is your mum ...?"

"She died when I was fifteen." Her hand began to shake. She clamped it with her other hand. "Dad remarried about two years later. And church ... became weird for me. Church was mum's place and seeing my stepmum there was just ... wrong. So I stopped going. I didn't realise I'd missed it." Fresh tears trickled down her cheek. She brushed it away. "I'm sorry," she said again.

Tilly passed her the tissues again. "It's okay. It's a sad thing. You're allowed to be upset."

Lara nodded and sniffed.

"So Christmas must be quite a funny time for you," said Tilly, quietly.

"You could say that." Lara blew her nose. "I used to spend some of it with Dad and stepmum, but then they had a baby ... and I stopped going. I think they were relieved, to be honest." The baby was her half-brother. That was far too weird. He felt more like a nephew. Her dad, who looked at the baby with such paternal pride, felt like a stranger. She sniffed. Thinking about this wasn't helping. She needed to think about something else. "How about you? What's Christmas like for you?"

"Oh, my parents aren't bothered. So long as we're home for the New Year, we can do what we like at Christmas," said Tilly, airily. "We always celebrated Christmas, even though we never did church. We tended to celebrate just about any religious holiday going. Any excuse for a party." She smiled. "Once we grew up, we all pretty much stopped going home for Christmas and spent it with girlfriends or friends."

"That must be quite liberating," said Lara.

"You'd think so," said Tilly. "But then, last year and the year before, I missed New Year. I was in Spain and didn't come home. My mum was not happy with me. I'm pretty sure she's tasked Vinnie with making sure I come home this year."

"Are you going to?"

Tilly shrugged. "Best, I suppose."

"Yeah. She is your mum. She loves you." Her mum had loved her too. She wondered if mum was watching her now. What did she see? Was she proud? Or was she judging her? Another tear ran down her cheek.

"Oh, hey. I'm sorry. Here I am complaining about my mum when you ... I'm so sorry," said Tilly. She put her arms around Lara and gave her another hug. Not too long. Just enough.

Tilly's phone buzzed as a WhatsApp call came through. She looked at it. "It's Vinnie," she said.

Lara nodded, indicating that she should take it.

"Vinnie," Tilly said, into the phone. "Yes, yes, I'm coming. Give me ten minutes." Whatever he said made her roll her eyes. "Loser. I'll see you in a bit." She put her phone away and looked earnestly at Lara. The kindness in her eyes nearly made Lara cry all over again. "Are you going to be okay?"

Lara nodded. It had been nice to have Tilly there, but it wasn't necessary. She was an adult. She could deal with her memories of her mother by herself. On the other hand, it was nice that Tilly cared. It had been a long time since anyone had got close enough to care. "Thank you for being here," she said. "You didn't have to."

"Oh, I had to," said Tilly, smiling. "I couldn't let you cry alone."

"Why?" said Lara. "You've been so kind to me."

Tilly shrugged. "I like you," she said. She looked away, at the door, then drew a firm breath. She turned back and hunkered down in front of Lara. She put her hands on Lara's knees. "Actually," she said, quietly. "I ... really like you." Her eyes met Lara's and there was no mistaking what she meant.

Lara's body responded with a spike of excitement. But her brain knew better. "I'm not ... looking for a relationship right now," she said.

"Neither am I," said Tilly. "I wasn't asking for any commitment. We're here. I fancy you. I think you don't hate me ..."

Lara shook her head. "I don't do that."

Tilly sighed. "Okay," she said. "In that case, I'm happy to just be your friend." She sat back and raised her hands in the air to emphasise the point. She smiled. "Are we okay?"

Lara nodded. "I'm sorry."

"Oh, don't be. It's fine." Tilly scrambled to her feet. "I'll be downstairs helping Vinnie and Tracey get the place ready for the party. You're welcome to join us."

"I'll come down in a minute."

As Tilly put her hand on the doorknob, Lara said, "Thank you. For understanding."

Tilly didn't reply. She smiled and let herself out.

Chapter 7

"How did the walk go?" Tilly's brother asked her when Angie finally left them alone. They were given the task of folding the napkins into fleur de Lys for the tables on Christmas lunch. The demonstration on how to do it had been exhaustive.

"It was going pretty well," said Tilly. "But then we went into the church to see the children's service and she started crying. Turns out her mum died when she was young ... and church was one of her things."

"Oh, that's sad," said Vinnie.

"It is." It was strange how heavy it made her feel. The artists' studio she had worked in did outreach work with a local orphanage. The kids came in and helped - not on the actual commission, but on smaller things. They made elements that would eventually end up as part of the whole. Their fingerprints were part of the uniqueness of the art. The expression on Lara's face when she heard the hymns reminded Tilly of those kids. All Tilly had wanted to do was to put her arms around her and protect her.

"Is she okay?"

Tilly nodded. "I think so. I spoke to her afterwards. She misses her mum. I mean, grief is like that. It gets you when you least expect it."

Vinnie gave her a sideways glance, as though to say 'what do you know about grief'? She ignored him and bent her head of her task. Lara had also said that she should appreciate her family while she still had them. She carefully placed the folded napkin in the box, nestled next to its neighbour, so that they all stood up neatly, like a delicate regiment.

"Have you seen Amma and Appachi recently?" she asked. "Are they okay?" She had spoken to them and there was always stuff on the family WhatsApp group, but she hadn't actually seen them in over a year.

"They're okay," Vinnie said. "Appachi's blood pressure is playing up a bit, so they've increased his pills. He's starting to look frail. Amma ... is the same as ever." He finished a napkin and took up another. "They're both really looking forward to seeing you."

"I bet." She rolled her eyes.

"Why do you do that?" said Vinnie. "They love you. You know they do."

"But there's always the judgement, isn't there? Every time I go home, they like to point out that I'm so immature. That I'm not settling down. Like I'm the failure in the family."

"They are struggling to understand you, that's all," said Vinnie. "You have to give them some leeway. You've pretty much rejected everything they believe to be the right way to be."

"Just because I'm gay," said Tilly. To her own surprise, her voice caught. It still hurt, even after all this time. Her parents tried to be supportive. Even in her angriest moments, she had to acknowledge that. But they just didn't get it.

Vinnie stopped working and looked earnestly at her. "Is that what you think? Really?"

Tilly frowned. "Well if it isn't that … why are they so down on me?"

"What have they been telling us all our lives?" said Vinnie.

"Study hard. Get good jobs. Work hard. Stay out of trouble," said Tilly. "Nothing you learn is wasted," she added in a passable impression of their mother's voice.

Vinnie gave a small laugh of recognition. "Yeah. Exactly. Hard work. Diligence. Stability. That sort of thing. Arun and I are both pretty conventional. Degree, job, career. They know how to deal with that. I mean, Arun even got married and had kids right on time. But you … Tilly they worry about you. They worry that you haven't got a base anywhere. They worry that you'll fall ill or be injured and have no way to support yourself. They worry that you'll need them and they'll be too old to help. They worry constantly about how you don't have a pension."

She stared at him. They nagged her about pensions and job security all the time. It hadn't occurred to her to think about where those worries came from. "Do they really think that they'll have to look after me if something goes wrong?"

"Well yes," said Vinnie. "You don't have any other support network. Or a place to call home. Until you do, they will always consider themselves to be your home."

"But they treat me like I'm still a child."

"Maybe you should try not acting like one."

She glared at her brother. "Bloody cheek!" she said. She put her hands on her hips. "Just because you've got the sort of job that lets you stay in one place and put down roots." As she said it, she knew she wasn't being fair. Work was hard to come by, for sure, but she didn't have to look for it in mainland Europe. There was no reason why she couldn't apply for projects in England. If Brexit happened, she might be forced to do so anyway. She could settle somewhere and make connections with local artists and become more established.

"I'm sorry," said Vinnie. "I didn't mean that. But I do mean it about the settling down. You don't have to stop exploring, just because you've made your bed in one place. It's just good to have a bed to call your own. Especially, if you're ill and you need to take to it..." he stopped and frowned. "Too far?"

Tilly pulled a face and shook her head. "You never did know when to stop."

Vinnie shrugged. He raised a quizzical eyebrow at her.

"Yes, yes fine. I see your point," she said. "But I can't settle down to the nine to five like you and Arun. I just can't."

"You don't have to. But you really should think about the future a bit. You can't keep drifting from one thing to another like this," said Vinnie. "And Amma and Appachi just want the best for you. They care about you. We all do."

Tilly didn't reply. For a minute or two, they worked in silence. When one box was filled with the delicately folded napkins, Vinnie moved it and put a new box in its place.

There are a knock. Tilly looked over her shoulder to see Lara, knocking on the door frame. "Can I help with anything?" she said, her voice small. Her eyes were dry now, but red rimmed. Tilly felt a pang of sadness. She wanted to hug her all over again.

"Oh, no, love," Angie said. "You're all right. You're a guest. You should enjoy your holiday. Can I get you something?"

"I'd like to help," said Lara. "I haven't really got anything else to do."

Tilly knew what Lara wasn't saying. There were things she didn't want to think about and being busy would take her mind off them.

"Oh go on, Angie, let her help," said Vinnie. "It's not like we're short of jobs to do." He looked past Angie at Lara. "If you don't mind helping Tilly with the napkin folding," he said. "I can go help the caterers unload. They've just pulled up."

"Have they?" said Angie. "Oh, about time!"

They both hurried off, leaving Lara and Tilly alone. Well, almost alone - there was a steady stream of people doing through the prep room. "Here, let me show you," said Tilly.

Lara gave her a grateful smile and came and stood next to her. It didn't take her long to get the hang of folding and they worked together in companionable silence.

Vinnie, Phil and Angie walked through the room and into the main kitchen carrying big trays of canapes. Tracey, in vinyl gloves and hairnet, took charge of things.

Tilly reached for a fresh napkin and her hand grazed the back of Lara's. The contact made her skin tingle. She glanced at her, to see her quickly look away. Tilly stifled a sigh. She'd tried. Lara said no. That was the end of that.

"I think we're nearly done," Tilly said.

"They look so neat and soft all lined up like this." Lara tucked the last napkin into the box and ran her fingertips over the soft napkin tops. "What's next?"

"You want more to do?" Tilly laughed.

"Sure. It's nice being part of something," said Lara.

"Well if you want to help." Angie appeared, as if by magic. The woman must have the ears of a bat. "You could help me do the veg for tomorrow."

"For the whole pub?" said Tilly, dismayed.

"No. For us. We'll all have Christmas brunch early, so that we can eat together before the pub opens. Phil's doing a roast. I need someone to do the veg."

"Of course," said Lara. "Show me what you need done."

"That would be brilliant, love. Thank you," said Angie. "It'll save me having to do it first thing in the morning." She got two aprons off a shelf and passed them to Lara.

Lara took one apron and passed the other to Tilly. "Is it usually busy on Christmas day?"

"Not so much during the day. We have a few regulars who come every year. People who are alone and so on. But it gets really busy towards the evening." Angie brought out a box with different vegetables bagged up in brown paper. "Here you do. I'll pop some pans out for you to put them into in a minute. Thank goodness there'll be no hot food to deal with tonight."

Lara looked puzzled.

"We get catering in from a local firm," said Angie. "They're doing nibbles. It takes the pressure off us and gives someone else a good Christmas."

"It's a complex ecosystem," Lara said, thoughtfully. She slipped the apron loop over her head and tied the ribbons at her waist. The apron was too long and it sagged at the top.

"Here, let me tie that up at the top for you," said Tilly.

"Would you, that'd be great." Lara dipped her head forward and lifted her hair out of her way. Tilly made two loops with the excess tie and made a small knot, so that the top of Lara's apron was pulled taut. Her fingers were so close to the nape of Lara's neck that she could feel the warmth radiating from her skin. The temptation to touch ... to gently stroke the soft down on the back of her neck was so tempting. But she had to resist. Consent wasn't something to be taken lightly. Tilly kept her focus, tied the apron strings and removed her hands.

"Thanks," said Lara. Her cheeks looked a little flushed. "Do you need me to do the same with yours?" she said.

"No. I seem to have a smaller apron than you," Tilly said. She didn't think she'd be able to cope with the whisper of Lara's fingers against her skin. Even the thought of it was making her throat dry.

They sat together at the prep table with a peeler each and got to work. Lara on potatoes, Tilly on carrots.

Something nagged in Tilly's mind as she peeled carrots. There was a half formed idea niggling away in her mind. "What did you mean when you said an ecosystem?" she said.

"What Angie said about someone else having a good Christmas," said Lara, who was cutting little Xs into sprouts. "The local businesses are interconnected. It's a ... pattern." She waved the paring knife vaguely. "I like patterns. Logistics."

"But being interconnected is what community is all about. Doesn't that mean that they're dependent on each other? Isn't that more vulnerable?"

"That's true," said Lara. "It means the system has more nodes where things can fail, but there's also more people to step up when things go wrong... so, it makes the collaboration as a whole stronger."

"So ... what you're saying is... it's nice to be part of something."

Lara laughed. "I guess I am."

Tilly looked around the room. They were on one side of the pub's professional kitchen. The metal surfaces were covered with trays and boxes. Angie was directing as Tracey and Vinnie put the relevant trays in the correct storage. Fridges, Freezers or shelf. Every so often, someone would crack a joke and they would all laugh. The atmosphere was warm and good humoured. It reminded Tilly of New Year's Eve at home, when she and her brothers did small chores for her parents. She had avoided going home for two New Years in a row now. She had remembered the questions and the judgemental silences, but she'd forgotten about the warmth.

Beside her, Lara seemed to be mellowing more by the second. If she routinely spent Christmas alone, she must not have had this for a long time either. They sat at the prep table, peeling and shopping. All around her was noise and bustle and general good humour. People from the village popped in for one thing or another. Was it still like this at home? While she was avoiding having to answer questions about her future, was this what she was missing?

There was a sudden "Yess!" from Vinnie.

Tilly looked up to see a young girl, a teenager, had arrived with a box. Balanced on top was a bag with 'Pat's Pantry' written on it. Vinnie, bless him, was always governed by his stomach.

The girl grinned. "Hot cinnamon buns," she said.

"I'll put the kettle on," said Phil, who had come in carrying a second box. "Let me just put this bread down."

By common agreement, everyone downed tools. Soon they were all sitting around the prep table, cups of tea in hand. Angie put a big plate of cinnamon rolls on the table. Tilly took two and passed one to Lara. She watched at Lara frowned and took a bite. Lara closed her eyes and made the softest 'mmm' sound. Her own cinnamon bun forgotten, Tilly stared as Lara chewed, swallowed and licked the sugar off her lips. Something inside her thrummed in response. Lara opened her eyes and their gazes met. For a second, she thought she saw a flare of want in Lara's eyes ... but then it was gone and Lara turned away to focus on her cinnamon bun again.

Tilly sighed. Oh well. Best to see what all the fuss was about. She took a bite. The bun was soft and sweet and cinnamony. It was just the balance of warmth and sweetness to make it a perfect comfort food. She wasn't a sweet tooth person, but even she had to agree that this was good.

"Oh," she said. "You were right Vinnie."

"See. Told you," her brother responded.

She looked at him, with his eyes shining, licking sugar off his fingers and burst out laughing. Some things never changed. She was very glad she'd agreed to come and spend some time with him.

Chapter 8

The pub was bustling by the time Lara came back downstairs that evening, wearing a borrowed Christmas jumper that made her look like a Christmas pudding. There were already a number of people there, mostly clustered around the bar or the pool table. The lights that Tilly had so artfully arranged, twinkled. With the snow coming down gently in the night outside, it felt like they were in a cocoon of light and warmth.

Later in the night, there would be a disco at the very small dance floor at one end of the pub, but it hadn't been switched on yet and with Christmas music playing, the pub looked timeless, as though it had been like this at Christmas time every year since it was built. She recognised a few of the faces already, because so many of them had dropped in to do various things in preparation for the party. This may be the pub Christmas event, but the whole village was involved in it. She waved to the girl from the bakery, who was there with a tall blonde young man and waved back. Lara spotted her friends standing around a high table. She stopped at the bar and got herself a glass of wine before she made her way towards them. As she got near, Tilly noticed her and waved. Vinnie and Tracey too, looked happy to see her. Her friends. She had known them for only twenty four hours, but she felt part of the small team. Tilly was... well, Tilly knew more about her than a lot of the people she worked with and saw every day. It was odd to know that. Odder still that she felt okay with it.

"We're trying to guess the weight of the Christmas pudding," Tilly said, pointing to the enormous pudding in a box, sitting on a table by the bar. "Tracey knows, but she's not telling."

"It would be unfair," said Tracey. "What would you do with it, if you won?"

"Eat it, obviously," said Vinnie. "Over several days."

Lara laughed and settled in next to Tilly to peer over her shoulder. Brother and sister returned to their earnest discussion.

"Is it always like this at Christmas?" Lara asked Tracey, partly just to make conversation.

Tracey smiled. "Yeah," she said. "It's very ... Trewton." They both looked round at the cosy space that was rapidly filling up.

"It's certainly a bit different to the parties in London, right?" said Tracey. "I wasn't really comfortable with them. Too bright, too many people. I felt always 'on', if you know what I mean."

Lara knew exactly what she meant. All the parties she normally went to were also networking opportunities. She was constantly on the lookout for potential new customers or allies. It was impossible to relax. "I guess you're never off duty when you're running a start-up."

Tracey nodded. "I think," she said, thoughtfully. "That we, especially us women in tech and other male dominated fields, we have to fight so hard for every inch of ground we gain, that sometimes it's hard to stop fighting. Even when we don't need to." Tracey tilted her head to the side. "I had forgotten that Christmas could be fun, to be honest. Until last year." She nudged Vinnie, who looked over at her. "Remember the party last year."

Vinnie put his arm around her and pulled her close to his side. "How could I forget?" he said warmly, and kissed her.

Tilly rolled her eyes. "Oh please."

"Anniversary at Christmas?" said Lara. "That's very organised. Only one set of presents to cover both."

Vinnie's eyes widened. "Yeah. Yes, exactly."

Tracey laughed and nudged him. "Oh relax," she said. "I didn't get you an anniversary present either."

"Phew."

THE EVENING WAS FUN. Since her phone was only buzzing to give her Christmas text messages, Lara turned it off and just let the evening take over. She was acutely aware of Tilly standing next to her. Aware of her deep and suggestive laugh, the hint of her perfume when she moved her arm, the beautiful lines of her face in profile. That morning, she had considered Tilly cute, but too risky a proposition. Now, it was all she could do to take her eyes off her. She told herself to stop being silly. She didn't have time for a relationship. Not now. And Tilly was really not her sort of person. Too unpredictable. Too ... out there.

Except, in the course of a day, she had got used to her. True to her word, Tilly had stopped flirting with her. There was camaraderie and maybe a hint of protectiveness about her, but nothing more. It astounded Lara that someone could turn the attraction on and off like that. Baffling.

However, it didn't stop Tilly flirting with other people. Right now, she was at the pool table. The bloke who had been watching them last night had approached and asked if they fancied a dance. They'd both politely declined and he'd jokingly said, 'How about a game of pool then?' Tilly had shrugged and said, 'Sure, why not?"

So now she a few feet away, playing pool with some random guy on a heavily tinselled pool table while Lara was finishing her glass of wine alone. The guy said something that made Tilly laugh. The laugh was surprisingly mucky. Lara watched as the guy put his hand on Tilly's arm. Tilly's laugh stopped abruptly. She shook off his hand, with a frosty smile.

Mine. The thought rose, primal and unbidden into Lara's head. The intensity of her jealousy surprised her. Where had that come from? As she watched, Tilly shook her head, clearly telling him she wasn't interested. He put his hand on her arm again. This time Tilly was firm in how she pushed it off.

Right. That was it. It didn't matter where the feelings came from. What mattered was that they were there. Lara drained her glass and marched over. She came up by the side of Tilly and put her hand on her shoulder.

Tilly jumped, then seeing who it was, smiled. Lara leaned up and put her chin on Tilly's shoulder. Together, they looked at the guy. He looked from one woman to the other. His eyes widened.

"Oh," he said. "Like that is it?" He stepped back, his hands held up. "Fair enough."

Lara gave Tilly's shoulder a gentle squeeze and felt the shoulder muscles move under her fingertips. Her gaze met Tilly's. Desire burned in Tilly's molten brown eyes. Oh. She hadn't turned those emotions off, then.

"Are you ... done here?" Lara said. Her voice came out unexpectedly thick and low.

Tilly nodded, slowly. "I think I am, yes."

There was a bark of laughter from one of the other men who had been leaning against a windowsill, watching the game of pool. "Way to misread the signs, mate," he said to the man who had been playing pool. "Unless you girls want some company?"

Tilly said, "Just a minute." She bounced the pool cue, so that it sat better in her hand and walked up to the guy at the windowsill, stepping close to him, pool cue still in hand. He leaned back, looking suddenly alarmed.

Tilly leaned closer, her eyes narrow. "Take over my game?" she said and thrust the pool cue towards him. He took it more out of surprise than volition.

As Tilly walked back, she clapped the first guy on the back and said, "Good game, Max," and winked at him.

He grinned back at her. "Yeah. Thanks. Merry Christmas, eh?"

"Merry Christmas to you too." Tilly reached Lara. "Shall we?"

They walked, shoulder to shoulder, out of the bar. As soon as they started up the stairs, Tilly took Lara's hand. Lara squeezed tightly, trying to communicate all her feelings through her fingers. They both ran up the stairs a little faster.

They had to drop hands so that Lara could unlock her door. Once inside, Tilly kissed her almost before she'd shut the door. She tasted of wine and cinnamon. Lara reached up and dug her fingers into Tilly's hair, feeling the tension as it strained against the bands tying it back. Tilly pulled her closer, one hand reaching under the dreadful jumper to graze her skin and set it on fire.

Lara pulled back so that she could tug the wretched jumper off.

"I thought you weren't interested," Tilly began.

"Shh." Lara pulled her close and kissed her again.

Tilly made noise, a deep sigh of satisfaction, and kissed her right back.

Chapter 9

Tilly woke up and breathed in perfume. Her body was curled around Lara's. Her arm was tucked around the other woman's warm middle. She smiled and lifted her head to plant a kiss on Lara's shoulder.

"Mm?" Lara stirred and looked over her shoulder at her.

"Hello," said Tilly. If Lara had looked pretty before, lying here, tousled and sleepy, she was positively glorious.

"Hey." Lara shifted position so that she was facing Tilly. She fussed with the bedding, pulling it up so that they were both snugly tucked it. Tilly caught Lara's hand and interlaced their fingers. Bringing their joined hands to her mouth, she kissed Lara's knuckles. Lara gave a contented sigh and closed her eyes.

Tilly examined their joined hands, felt the weight of Lara's smooth palm against her own rough one. She examined Lara's fingers, with the darker bands at the joints, light brown against her own sun baked brown. They fitted together so well. When Lara had turned her down that first time, she had thought that was it. End of story. And yet here they were.

"Can I ask a question?" said Tilly.

"Sure." Lara sounded sleepy.

"What changed your mind?"

"What?"

"You said no before. What changed your mind?"

Lara opened her eyes. "Something Tracey said ... I realised that I've been so busy fighting for everything at work that I'd forgotten I didn't need to fight you... or how I feel about you."

Oh. That was lovely. "How do you feel about me?"

"I like you." Lara's eyes crinkled in a smile. "I thought that was pretty obvious. Considering."

Tilly chuckled and saw Lara's eyes light up in response. "I like you too," she said, grinning. "In case it wasn't obvious."

Lara kissed her. "So you said. You have no idea how nice it is to know beforehand, you know."

"Oh, I know," said Tilly. "I find it just wastes lots of time being circumspect. I like to be more direct."

Lara raised herself up on one elbow and looked at her. "And ... you said you weren't after anything serious..." It sounded like a question.

"Nope," said Tilly. "I don't really do commitment. And you're busy. But you're here and I'm here and we are great together... so why not have fun for the next few days, right?" Because she was watching, Tilly saw the look of relief pass across Lara's face, just before she leaned in to kiss her. It was good to know they were on the same page.

"You're so ... sorted. You know what you want. You go for it. I so envy you," Lara said.

Tilly snorted. "I'm not sorted. Just easily bored."

Lara frowned.

"I don't mean that I'm bored of you," Tilly added quickly. "But I don't generally stay in one place for very long."

Lara was still frowning, as though trying to work out if she was being insulted.

"Let's not talk about that, right now," said Tilly. She stroked the beautiful curve of Lara's cheek. "It's well past midnight now, I should think. Merry Christmas." She leaned in and kissed her. Then kissed her some more.

WHEN LARA AND TILLY went downstairs for breakfast together, Lara felt like everyone was giving them knowing glances. "I think they all know," she muttered to Tilly.

"Relax," Tilly whispered back. "Of course they know. It's a village. Everyone knows everything." She grinned. "People hook up at Christmas parties all the time. Don't stress."

They were late, so there weren't many people eating. Given that there had been a fairly major party the night before, the pub didn't look too bad. Angie and Phil had blocked off the back of the pub and cleared the front part, so that the overnight guests could have breakfast.

"We'll be having early Christmas lunch," Angie informed them when she brought them some toast and coffee.

"Can we help with anything?" said Tilly.

Angie looked from one to the other. "If you like," she said. "And then you're coming to Christmas lunch. We don't open until after lunch today. People who come round for Christmas lunches, tend to come round mid-afternoon, so that they finish lunch in time to catch the Queen's speech."

After quickly polishing off a slice of toast, Lara followed Tilly as she carried the breakfast things into the kitchen. The back of the pub smellled heavenly. Clearly, the roast was already on.

"Ah good," said Angie. "Would you mind helping clear up the pub and setting up the tables for later?" She showed them where the table decorations and carefully folded napkins were and then sent them off with cleaning clothes to get the pub ready.

THEY HAD CHRISTMAS dinner well just before noon, all crammed around the big prep table in the kitchen, so that they didn't mess up the carefully set out tables in the pub itself. Lara sat next to Tilly, wearing that awful Christmas jumper again. Tilly moved her chair closer so that she could hook her foot around Lara's. They bumped elbows when they moved. They pulled a cracker between them and for the first time in years, Lara wore the paper hat. She had expected to feel awkward at this meal table with relative strangers, but Angie and Phil didn't seem to have any reservations about a guest joining them.

No one drank much, because most of them would be working later that day. There were plenty of jokes and the food was excellent.

At one point Vinnie told everyone a story about Tilly's first attempt at making Yorkshire pudding. Phil gravely explained to Tilly where she'd gone wrong, which, to Lara's surprise, Tilly took with good humour.

"It's the first time we've had Christmas dinner together since ... well, since I was a teenager," Tilly said to Vinnie.

Angie shook her head. "Are you sure your parents don't mind you spending it here?"

"Oh no," said Tilly. "They'll be in London, partying. We never really did family Christmas dinner anyway. The olds used to drag us down to London to hang out with their friends."

"We used to go to the Sri Lankan restaurant for lunch and then there would always be a party at some auntie's house," said Vinnie. "It'd be a house full of Sri Lankan people and the party would go on for ever."

"That sounds like fun," said Tracey.

"It was. Especially when we were small," said Tilly. "Lots of kids all together."

"Ha. Like you behaved yourself," said Vinnie. "You used to escape and tag along to the pub with us older kids."

"Yeah," said Tilly, with a complete lack of contrition.

"You owe me for covering for you," said Vinnie.

Tilly patted his arm. "You're a good brother."

"What about you, love?" Angie asked Lara.

"My ... Dad and stepmum do Christmas with my ... er... brother. He's just a baby." Talking about this was uncomfortable. Christmas was a time for happy families. Her story of not belonging in her dad's house felt desperately out of place. She looked down at her plate. Tilly gave her hand a gentle squeeze. Lara glanced across and gave her a grateful smile.

There was a short pause and Angie said, "Well, you're very welcome here, love."

Everyone said 'cheers' or 'amen to that' and warmth blossomed in Lara's chest. Here, in the midst of virtual strangers, she felt included in a way she hadn't done in a long time.

"Pass the gravy," said Phil. "Not you, our Tracey. I don't trust you with sloppy things. Someone else."

Vinnie laughed and passed the gravy boat.

"I'd have been very careful not to spill it," Tracey protested in a wounded voice.

"I'm sorry, love," said Phil, eyes twinkling at her.

Tracey smiled fondly back.

Lara let their conversation and laughter wash over her as she sipped her glass of wine. This was fun, but it wasn't how life was every day. In a few hours, all this would be cleared up - this dishes washed, the table scrubbed. Phil and Angie would go back to work in the pub and it would be like it never happened.

She was distracted from her thoughts by Tilly gently stroking her hand. When she looked up, Tilly mouthed 'okay?' to her. She nodded and turned her hand over so that their fingers could link. All this might end in a few hours, but for now, it was wonderful. She should really just enjoy the moment.

AFTER A FLURRY OF ACTIVITY clearing up, with Christmas jingles playing loudly in the pub kitchen, the non-staff members were shooed out of the kitchen so that Angie could get the pub open. Lara borrowed a coat from the stash and ventured outside with Tilly to walk off some of the food. They walked down past the shops towards the brook that ran past. There was a path by the bridge, that let down to the water-side. They stopped at the bench and sat down, shoulders touching.

"This is the best Christmas I've had in a long time," Lara said.

Tilly looked thoughtful for a moment. "Me too," she said. "I've had Christmas in Spain and in Italy. Once in a commune in Wales. None of them have been as nice as this." She smiled. "I think I'll blame it on you being here."

"You do that," said Lara.

Tilly laid her head on Lara's shoulder. They sat there, watching the water babble past. There wasn't much sun, but it wasn't snowing, at least. It was cold enough for their breath to fog in front of them, but the walk and the enormous meal was keeping Lara warm. Or maybe it was just the company. Lara kissed the top of Tilly's head and sighed happily.

"Are you going to call you dad?" Tilly said, quietly.

And that killed the mood.

Lara sighed, in a very different way this time. "I suppose I should," she said.

"It's Christmas," said Tilly. "He'll be glad to hear from you."

"I doubt that."

"Oh, come on. It must be weird for him too. He's got this new family, who are the new centre of his life …. Which is where you used to be. He's got to learn how to interact with you as an adult, rather than as a child. Plus there's the whole queer thing, which, it sounds like, he didn't deal with very well… It's a lot of fundamental things that have shifted there."

"They shifted for me too," said Lara. She pushed away. "It's not been easy."

Tilly put a hand on her arm. "Hey. I know it's not been easy for you. I can see how much it hurts you. I'm just saying that if you both choose to focus on your own pain, you're going to keep each other away and that's sad. Give him an opening. See if he takes it."

"It's all very well for you," said Lara. "Your family sound amazing. What is your problem anyway? Why do you keep your parents away?"

"I don't," said Tilly. She didn't meet Lara's eye. "It's completely different. I just need to sort myself out. Then I can go back and play perfect daughters."

"Sort yourself out? How?"

Tilly shook her head. "Look, it doesn't matter, okay. What does matter is you. You should call your dad. Just say merry Christmas."

"He could call me," said Lara.

"What? Here? In the village that time forgot? There's no mobile signal. He could call and you'd never know."

She couldn't argue with that. Had her father tried to call? Lara grimaced. She should find out. And Tilly was right. Rather than waiting stubbornly for her father to apologise, she could be the one to open the door to reconciliation. She swore under her breath. "I'm going to have to call him, aren't I?"

"Probably best," said Tilly. She kissed Lara's cheek. "It'll be okay. You'll feel better for having done it. And even if you don't ..." Her voice dropped low. "I'm sure I can take your mind off things."

The suggestion in her voice shot heat through Lara. She shook her head. "Low blow," she said, smiling.

Tilly raised her eyebrows.

Lara laughed. "Fine," she said. She stood up. "Although, I don't know why you care."

Tilly jumped to her feet. "I care because I can tell it's eating away at you. I want you to be happy."

"Aw," said Lara. "That's sweet."

"Yeah." Tilly wrinkled her nose. "I'm cute like that."

LARA HAD TO WAIT UNTIL they got back into the pub's Wi-Fi range to make the call. Even her data connection was patchy in the village. Leaving Tilly downstairs, she went to her room and sat on the end of her bed. She checked the time. The Queen's speech was due to start soon, so they would probably be at the end of their meal now and if they needed it, they could use the Queen as an excuse to get off the phone. She took a deep breath and hit call.

Her stepmother answered the phone.

"Hi. It's... Lara," she said. "I'm just calling to say Merry Christmas."

There was a beat of silence before her stepmother said, "Oh, that's nice. Merry Christmas to you too. Let me just get your dad."

Lara sat and waited, listening to her own breathing. Finally, her dad came on the one line. "Lara. Happy Christmas."

"Merry Christmas, dad. Did you have a nice day so far?"

"Yes, yes, thanks."

"And how's baby Henry?"

"He's good. Doing really well." She could hear his tone of voice lightened when he spoke about Henry. Did he ever sound like that when he talked about her? She listened to him while he gave her a rundown of what Henry could do now, with pride in every syllable. Henry was 18 months old. Walking was only to be expected, surely.

"Dad, I went to church yesterday," she said.

He stopped mid sentence. "Did you? That's wonderful."

"It reminded me of mum," she said.

Her dad sighed. "Yes," he said. "Church always reminded me of her too. Is ... is that why you stopped going?"

"Partly, I guess," she said. "Dad, does church no longer remind you of her?"

He cleared his throat. Buying time, she guessed.

"I still think of your mother from time to time," he said. "I haven't forgotten her. I just found a way to hold other things in my heart alongside her." He cleared his throat again. "And you."

She had assumed... actually, didn't know what she had assumed, but she'd taken his new relationship as a betrayal of sorts. She'd viewed everything about his stepmother through that prism. Her father was only human. He would have got lonely and needed company, just like anyone else would. Wrapped up in her own pain, she hadn't seen that.

"Lara?" he said. "I do still love you, you know. I just love other people too."

"I know dad," she said, quietly.

"I'm glad," he said. "And I'm really glad you called. It means a lot."

"I'm glad I called too."

"So, what's new with you? How's London?"

"I'm stuck in the middle of nowhere in Yorkshire, at the moment," she said. "I came up here to meet a client and couldn't get home."

"Oh no. That's terrible."

"Actually, it could have been worse," she smiled. "The pub I'm staying in is nice and I met someone I like."

"A young man?"

"No dad, a girl."

"Ah." There it was. The disappointment. "Well, it was nice to talk to you, Lara. I'm very happy you called. Merry Christmas."

Lara closed her eyes. "Yes. Merry Christmas to you too, dad."

After she hung up, she sat and stared into space for a very long time. She couldn't figure out exactly how she felt, but it wasn't the usual anger. There was sadness there, tempered by something else. Understanding, perhaps.

Her dad didn't like it that she preferred women. He probably never would. But he still loved her. He hadn't disowned her and in his own way, he was trying. That would have to be all for now. She stood up, put her phone in her pocket and went downstairs to find Tilly.

Chapter 10

The trains were running again! Lara was sitting on the bed, checking train times on her phone. It was Boxing Day and the world was functioning again. Thank goodness, she could get back to her life.

She looked up to where Tilly was lying on the bed reading an old romance novel from Tracey's collection. Going back to her real life meant leaving Tilly. Their 'relationship', if you could call it that, was a strictly temporary affair. They were both very clear about that. For a second she indulged in a fantasy where Tilly came back to London with her ... but that wouldn't happen. Lara had a business to run. It took up all her time and energy. Tilly was a bright, fast moving, firework. She would never be content to be tied down to a regular job and she would never be happy to play second fiddle to Haulistic Solutions.

So Lara studied Tilly, absorbing the image of her into her memory, so that she could picture her for days to come. That lovely hair, those nimble artist's fingers, that smile - sometimes mischievous, sometimes downright wicked. A small sigh escaped her.

The sound made Tilly look up. "What?" she said. Her eyes crinkled at the edges and Lara felt the sense of loss so keenly that she had to blink back sudden tears.

She cleared her throat. "The trains are running again," she informed Tilly quietly.

"Oh." Tilly's face fell. She turned her book over and laid it face down on the bed. "So... what does that mean?"

"Well, it means I can go home," said Lara. She lowered her phone. "I have to go home."

"So soon?" Tilly pushed herself into a sitting position. "I mean, I know your stay was only temporary, but do you have to go right away?"

"I've been living out of a bag - with hastily bought cheap knickers and borrowed jumpers. I have one pair of trousers. This isn't my life. I would really, really like to go home," Lara said. Despite her own misgivings, she said, "But it doesn't have to be the end for us. You could come with me."

"I ... really should go to my mum and dad's," Tilly said, not meeting her eyes.

"Come to me afterwards. You could stay in my flat." Lara opened the one drawer she was using and scooped the contents into her bag. She threw them in with slightly more force than was necessary. Why was she even having this discussion? She knew how it was going to go. She didn't have time for a relationship. They would have to part at some point.

"What would I do while you were at work?" said Tilly, distantly.

"I don't know. What would you do if you were elsewhere?" Lara unplugged her phone charger. Wouldn't do to lose that.

"I would probably be searching for the next commission," said Tilly. "To go somewhere abroad."

Lara stopped and faced her. "You're going to keep moving?"

Tilly leaned forward and took Lara's hands. "I can't settle down and be the stable girlfriend, with the stable job. I just can't. I have to keep moving. It's who I am."

Lara sighed. "I have to work. Haulistic Solutions is my baby. If I don't stick with it and give it my all, it'll never fly and I'll never forgive myself."

Tilly nodded. "I feel the same way about my art and my freedom. So ... I guess this is it?"

The pressure behind her eyes was unbearable. Lara dropped Tilly's hands so that she could wipe away the tears that were gathering.

Tilly promptly leaned across and handed her the box of tissues.

Lara took a tissue and dried her eyes. She made a noise that was half sniff and half laugh. "What is it about you that makes me cry all the time?"

"I have that effect on people," said Tilly, her voice hoarse. "It's a gift."

"Oh." Lara threw her arms around Tilly and pulled her close. She buried her face in the other woman's hair. "Oh Tilly."

"I'll miss you." Tilly's voice was muffled against her neck.

"I'll miss you too."

They drew apart so that they could look at each other. A tear escaped down Lara's cheek. Tilly wiped it away with her thumb.

"It's been ... amazing," Tilly said, continuing to stroke Lara's cheek with her thumb. "But neither of us can make a commitment. We agreed at the start. Nothing's changed, really."

Lara bit her lip. "No," she said. "Nothing has."

Tilly kissed her. A last, hot, salty kiss. When they parted, there was a sense of finality to it.

Lara took a step back, gathering her feelings close, so that she could go back to being her old, business-like herself. "I ... er ... have to go down to settle up and order a taxi. Do you want to...?"

Tilly shook her head. "No," she said. "I don't think I can." She slipped off the bed and picked up her shoes, which were lying on the floor. "You go ahead. I'll just go to my room."

"Right." Lara backed towards the door, her laptop bag raised in front of her. She grabbed her coat off the hook. "Yes. I'll see you then."

When she reached the door, Tilly said, "Merry Christmas, I guess. And ... you know, Happy New Year." She was still looking at her shoes.

"You too." Lara stepped out into the landing and closed the door behind her. For a moment, she thought her chest was going to split open with the pain. She took a deep breath and pulled herself upright. No. This was how it had to be. Her few days with Tilly had been a fun interlude, but now she had to get back to the real world. She put her bag down and pulled on her coat, which was looking very sorry for itself now. If the dry cleaner couldn't rescue it, she'd have to find time to go buy a new coat before January. It didn't do to wander around looking scruffy. She had a business to run.

TILLY WANTED TO CRY. The taxi, with Lara in it, climbed up the hill. Tilly was currently in her room, with her face pressed against the cold window, so that she could see the light gleam off the car roof. She didn't blame Lara for leaving. She herself had been clear, right from the start, that she couldn't do commitment. It was good that Lara wanted the same thing. If they hadn't been in agreement, then their brief fling would never have happened. Thank goodness Lara was too busy to want a longer term relationship.

And now... well, there was always this lull when she broke up with someone. She should have been expecting it, really.

The car crested the hill and disappeared over to the other side. Tilly moved away from the window and sat on the bed under the eaves. So that was it. End of the affair with Lara. She sighed and lay down. Lara was incredible. Beautiful, smart and driven. From the conversation between Lara and Tracey, it was obvious that they both worked in a field that didn't make life easy for women and there Lara was, heading up her small tech company, making it work. It had cost her a lot of time and energy and, by the looks of it, all of her chill. It was the prickliness that had first attracted Tilly. To find a layer of vulnerability so close beneath it had been a surprise.

For a brief second, she'd wondered if things could be different. If she could stay in London and Lara could maybe work less. But clearly, that wasn't a realistic idea. No. It had been a wonderful fling, but long term, they would have destroyed each other. Tilly would eventually hate Lara for tying her down and Lara would blame them both for her beloved Haulistic Solutions not taking the world by storm. Logically, she knew all that, but it still hurt. She curled her fingers into her palm and felt the absence of Lara's hand in hers. The sense of loss roared in her veins.

Tilly sighed. Sitting here thinking about wasn't making her feel any better. She needed to do something. Something physical. What she really wanted to do was to tear the world down and burn it for making her feel this way. But that wasn't practical. Still, she needed to move. Maybe go she could go for a walk. She had been so wrapped up in Lara, she hadn't taken the time to explore this village. It would be a shame to have spent so much time here and not ever see the place properly. Yes. A walk. That seemed like a good idea.

A few minutes later, she was bundled up warm and heading out into the crystal clear day. She paused to drag in a deep breath and feel the air tingle in her throat. Vinnie wasn't wrong when he said this place was beautiful. With the snow still dusting the rooftops and ledges, it looked like a Christmas card with glitter on it. She looked up at the hills that climbed up beyond the village. The contours of the hillside were so textured that she wanted to reach out and stroke it. Her hands itched to capture it. She must file it away for future reference. She could use it in a sculpture, maybe. Or even in a painting. She turned away from the road that had taken Lara out of the village and headed towards the church. She walked around it, until she found a vantage point that gave her a clear view of the church, with the hills behind it. If only she had a sketchbook right now.

She took out her phone and took a couple of photos. Still no signal. Putting the phone away, she concentrated on the church. There was a certain bleakness to the rough-hewn stone and the skeletal trees around it, but it was softened by the snow. Someone had built a snowman. Probably the kids from the Christmas Eve service. Ah crap. Thinking about the service reminded her of Lara. Tilly sighed. She'd liked Lara. Normally, she faced breakups with relative equanimity, but this stung like a wound. Once, in art school, she'd cut herself on a very sharp scalpel. The cut had been so fast and so clean that for a minute or two, she hadn't even realised she was hurt. And then with the blood there came the stinging pain. That was what this felt like. A cut that was so sharp that it had taken a few minutes for the full impact to hit.

Being without Lara made her feel … odd. Without her, Tilly felt unbalanced and even more at odds with the world than usual. What was it about Lara that had got so far under her skin? She'd only known her for a few days, so why did it feel like they'd known each other forever? She thought about how she'd held Lara while she cried, that overwhelming need to look after her and make things better. Tilly was not normally given to being protective of people. She rarely stuck around long enough to get that close.

She was still thinking about it, elbows on the top of the low wall, when Vinnie came out to find her.

"Angie said Lara checked out," said Vinnie, leaning on the wall beside her. "You okay?"

"Why wouldn't I be?" Tilly said, her eyes still on the church.

"You seemed close. She made you smile," said Vinnie. "So, what happened? Are you going to keep in touch?"

"She left, Vin. It's over. You know I don't really do long term stuff."

"I have never understood why not."

Tilly gave her brother, Mr serial monogamist, a sidelong glance. "No. You wouldn't."

Vinnie made a small huffing noise. They stood side by side, staring at the church, for a few minutes. Tilly suddenly wanted to cry.

"Can I tell you something?" Vinnie said, suddenly. "Don't tell Amma."

"Sure."

"I'm going to ask Tracey to marry me."

Tilly turned to look at him. "But you've only been together a year."

Vinnie shrugged. "I know. But I think she's the one."

She studied his earnest face for a minute. Both her brothers tended to be all or nothing kind of guys. Vinnie had been totally devoted to his last girlfriend too. "You thought your last girlfriend was the One. You even bought her a ring."

Vinnie sighed and shook his head. "I know. But this feels ... completely different. Tracey makes me feel ... like I'm a hundred percent myself and that's okay. Do you know what I mean?"

Oddly enough, she did. Lara had made her feel like that. She hadn't needed to tone anything down or ramp anything up. She just was who she was and it had been enough. She hadn't even had to show her art work to impress Lara. No. She couldn't think about that. She tore her mind away. "How can you be so sure?" she said to Vinnie. "It's a big commitment. How can you know you're doing the right thing?"

"I don't," he said. "I just believe I am. No one ever knows for certain, do they?"

"But isn't that terrifying?"

Vinnie frowned. "Yes. Doesn't mean you shouldn't do it."

"But what if it goes wrong and you regret it?"

"What if it doesn't go wrong and I get to be this happy for the rest of my life?"

Tilly stared at him for a minute, then shook her head. "It will be okay. It always is, for you," she said. Even she could tell she sounded like a petulant child. "You always land on your feet. You and Arun are good at everything."

Vinnie laughed. "No I'm not."

She shot him an angry glare, full of frustration from a childhood of watching her brothers excel while she struggled to keep up.

"I'm not, honestly. Neither is Arun."

She snorted. "Could have fooled me." She looked away. But she couldn't let it drop. All the pain she was feeling had to go somewhere. She aimed it at Vinnie. "Do you know what it's like being the one who couldn't get anything above a B ... when you two got A grades without any fuss? The only thing I was good at was art. Thank goodness I was very good at that. It's no fun being the thick one." And now she was back to feeling sorry for herself.

"You're not thick," said Vinnie. "And I'm not that clever. I worked my butt off for those grades."

"You and Arun, you just flew through whatever you did."

"Not true," said Vinnie. "I refer you to GCSE French."

She remembered vaguely that he hadn't enjoyed that. "You passed."

"Only just."

"Okay, well Arun then. He was good at everything he did."

"That's because he didn't do anything he might be bad at. Do you remember when he was mad keen on football?"

She thought back. No. She couldn't remember Arun even watching football. He tended to sneer at it. "No. He hates football."

"Maybe you were too little to remember," said Vinnie. "He decided he wanted to play football, so mum took us both to soccer club. He was pretty bad, but he kept going for a few weeks and then he got to play in an actual match." Vinnie grinned, expression far away as he remembered. "Oh, he was terrible. Worse than me, even! He got his arse kicked." He shrugged, still grinning. "The next day he claimed football was stupid and he hated it. And that was that."

"Wow," said Tilly. This was exactly what she needed to take her mind off things. Arun bashing. "I'm trying to imagine Arun being bad at something."

"He just never does anything if there's a chance he'll be bad at it." Vinnie gave her shoulder a little nudge. "You two are quite similar in that way."

"What?" She was nothing like her stuffy, over-achieving big brother. "How dare you?"

"It's true though, isn't it?" said Vinnie. "I remember. You'd try something once and then, if you weren't immediately good at it, you'd say 'nope. Too boring' and drop it. Thank goodness you were good at art the first time round!"

"That's not true," she said, huffily.

"It is," said Vinnie. "Wait, is that why you don't stay in one place for very long? Are you afraid that things might not work out, so you move on rather than having to say you tried and failed? That's it, isn't it?"

"Has anyone ever told you you're an annoying tit?"

"Yes. You have. I'm your big brother. Annoying you is part of my job description. Anyway, I'm right aren't I?"

She wanted to snap that he wasn't, but ... wasn't he? She thought about Diane's offer for her to step in and take the artist's place on next year's project. What exactly was it that was stopping her taking it? It would be a nice, paying job for eighteen months... she would be in England, with friends. Okay, it was sculpture rather than painting, but she'd done sculpture before. She didn't have any commitments anywhere else. She'd wanted to refuse because her gut instinct was to refuse. But was her gut instinct always right? She scowled.

"Tilly?" said Vinnie, his voice suddenly worried.

If her gut was wrong about that? What else was it wrong about? She'd gone into her short fling with Lara assuming she wouldn't want to hang around to see Lara longer term. What if she was wrong? Is that why she felt this wrongness with the world?

No, there were reasons for her assumption that her thing with Lara was only temporary. They'd only met because they happened to be spending a few days in the same place. Their worlds would never have collided if the trains hadn't been cancelled... so what? Plenty of people met by chance, when things weren't exactly right for them to settle down. But they made changes. Realigned themselves so that they could be the person they were meant to be with. Sometimes that wasn't easy, but it had to be worth it ... otherwise people wouldn't do it. Tracey had moved to Leeds to be near Vinnie. Amma had moved from Scotland to England to be with Appachi. For them, it had been worth it.

And what if Vinnie was right? What if she really was running away from things and because she was scared of giving difficult things a chance? Could she have made it work with Lara, if she'd just been willing to compromise? But Lara didn't want to either... She had a fledgling business to get off the ground. From conversations she'd overheard between Lara and Tracey, Haulistic Solutions was at a tricky stage. Lara had to focus. Lara needed someone who could give her the space to keep pushing at her business. Someone who could fade into the background because she had her own things to do. Someone who was safety valve for her to let off steam. In a moment of clarity, Tilly saw that she could be that person.

When she was fully immersed in a project, she focused. Having her own passion, helped her understand Lara's. Perhaps they weren't as mismatched as they first appeared. Perhaps ... they were exactly what each other needed...

"Tilly, are you okay?"

She looked at her brother. "Did I just make a terrible mistake Vinnie?"

Thankfully, he didn't need her to explain. "About Lara?" He frowned. "Do you like her? Or were you just messing around?"

"I ...thought I was messing about, but I think I really like her. I miss her. I mean, more than usual..." Without thinking, she curled her hand against her heart.

"Does she like you, do you think?"

Tilly recalled the look on Lara's face. Lara had been angry ... and hurt. Despite Tilly's very clear statement when they got together, Lara had still been hurt when she'd said goodbye. "Yes..." she said thoughtfully. "I think she likes me too." And she'd let her go, just like that. Without a fight or even a second of consideration. Just because she was too scared of things going wrong to even give it a chance to go right. "Oh shit." She looked up at her brother. "Vinnie, I've screwed up. What do I do?"

Vinnie frowned. "Go after her," he said. "What time was her train?"

"I don't know."

"Okay," said Vinnie. "I'll drive you. You check the train times."

They ran back to the pub, pausing only for Tilly to dart upstairs to grab her bag and for Vinnie to tell Tracey where they were going.

Tilly jumped in and clicked her seat belt into place. "The train left ten minutes ago," she said.

Vinnie chewed the inside of his cheek. "What do you want to do?"

"Can I borrow some money? I'm going to London. I don't have her number, but I know what her business is called. I'll find her."

Vinnie put the car into gear and looked over his shoulder to reverse out. "How can you not have her number?"

"There wasn't any point, was there? There's no phone reception here and I knew exactly where she was the whole time."

"Hmm," said Vinnie, as he pulled the car out of the car park. "Well, let's hope you catch her. I'd better lend you more than just the train fare."

HUDDERSFIELD STATION was relatively quiet. There was another train heading south in a few minutes. She would have to change trains in Sheffield. Tilly paced up and down. On the open platform, the wind was cutting. She was glad she'd wrapped up warm. She thought of Lara in her thin coat that looked amazing, but was too thin to be of any use. Poor Lara would be frozen in this weather.

Vinnie had decided to wait with her. He stood a short distance away, almond croissant in one hand, coffee in the other.

"What if you can't get hold of her through her work?" he said. "Where will you stay?"

"Dunno." Tilly stopped pacing. "Holiday Inn?"

"You could try Arun's."

"No way. I'd have to explain."

Vinnie sighed. "Hold this." He handed her the coffee, stuck the croissant in his mouth and pulled out his phone. After a minute or two, he took the pastry out of his mouth and said, "I've moved a few hundred quid into your account. I expect you to pay me back."

She handed him his coffee back. "I will. I promise. If I take this thing that Diane was talking about, I'll have some decent money for a bit."

"What thing that Diane was talking about?"

Oh crap. She shouldn't have mentioned that just yet. If she told him the details he would start pressuring her to take it and she really needed to think things through properly. "Oh, just a project," she said. "Nothing's certain yet. It was just an idea."

"Something in the UK?" Vinnie took a sip of his coffee. Although his voice was muffled, she could still hear the keen edge to it.

"Don't tell Amma."

He shook his head.

"Diane put in an application for a community art grant. It had money for a sculptor in it, but the person she had lined up has a family crisis and can't do it … so … she could look into substituting me instead. She doesn't know if it's allowed," she added quickly. If she decided against it, she needed a plausible reason. "So it might come to nothing."

"And you said … what?" Vinnie's eyes were narrow. He knew her well enough to see what she wasn't saying.

"I'm thinking about it," Tilly said.

Vinnie nodded slowly. "You know you'll be really good at it, right?" he said.

"You think?" She was a good enough artist. She could make a good go of it. The question was did she want to? Travelling around from project to project had sunk so far into her bones that she wasn't sure she could stop. But she had to give it proper thought. Staying in one place meant that she had a chance to be with Lara and she really, really wanted that.

"Of course," said Vinnie. "I've been to all of the shows you did in this country. You're very talented."

"Huh. I don't think you've ever said that before."

"Haven't I?" Vinnie looked genuinely surprised. "I guess me showing up to all your exhibitions didn't give you a clue?"

She laughed. "I suppose it should have." There was a general movement among the people on the platform. She looked up the line. The train was coming. "Oh, here goes," she said.

"Good luck," said Vinnie. "Hope you find her."

Suddenly, she was tense. She nodded and hitched her handbag firmly onto her shoulder.

"And remember," said Vinnie. "When you're a rich and famous artist, I'm the supportive brother who always believed in you."

"Muppet," she said, fondly. He was always her favourite brother anyway.

The train stopped. She joined the crush of people around the doors. Once inside, she moved along until she found a seat by the window. It was on the opposite side to the platform, so she had to crane her neck to see Vinnie. He waved, even though he probably couldn't see her and then walked towards the stairs to go back.

Tilly clutched her handbag on her lap and looked ahead. Lara was out there somewhere. She just had to find her.

Chapter 11

Lara's determination sustained her until she was on the train. The train had been busy enough that she'd had to stand, but luckily she'd managed to nab a seat when someone got off. With her laptop bag tucked safely at her feet, she stared out of the window, at the countryside whizzed past taking her further and further away from Tilly. The separation weighed on her, each mile seeming to make her heart heavier. Her time with Tilly, in the little bubble of Trewton Royd was wonderful, but it had it end. She'd known that it would hurt when they parted.

Lara sighed. When she got home, she would have a good cry and then try and get on with things. She would write this episode off as an adventure precipitated by bad weather and terrible trains. No one at work needed to know that anything had happened at all. She could say she was stuck in a godforsaken pub in the middle of nowhere, forced to sit in her room and watch Netflix because there was bugger all else to do. It was the lousiest of Christmases and that would be the end of that.

She rehearsed it in her head. Yes. That was plausible. If they asked her what she did for her Christmas meal, she could say she'd got something from the pub downstairs. Which would be true. Her breath hitched. Except ... no one would ask. They would assume that her Christmas was exactly as boring as she was pretending it to be and not think to dig any deeper. Why would they? Her life was completely consumed by work. Even when it wasn't, she liked to give the impression that it was, so that they wouldn't see any chinks in her go-getting businesswoman armour. Tracey was right. She spent her whole life fighting and it was exhausting. But was that wrong? The only time she'd loosened her hold on herself long enough, was in Trewton Royd and it had ended up with her adding sadness and regrets to her emotional load.

She chewed on her lip and looked out of the window at the snowy countryside sliding past. Oh, but it had been wonderful. Christmas day, despite the bustle in the pub, had been warm and so full of laughter. It had been years since she'd felt so much a part of something. The feeling of connection with her mother in the church had been profound and unexpected. Even the conversation with her father had been less awkward than before. At the centre of it all, was Tilly.

Tilly, who wore her affection lightly, who talked to and flirted with everyone; who appeared on the outside to be the most open person in the world, but kept the core of herself carefully locked away. Tilly, who made Lara feel at peace with herself.

But she was also the Tilly who had told her in no uncertain terms that there would be no future. Lara had only agreed to their liaison because of that. Well, that and a few other attractions. When it came to the crunch, Tilly hadn't made it awkward. They had parted quietly and neatly, just as they'd agreed in the first place.

Lara sighed. She missed Tilly already. They hadn't said goodbye, or exchanged numbers, although Tilly wouldn't be hard to find. There couldn't be many Thilini Fonsekas who worked in the arts. She could just Google ... She picked up her phone and did just that.

And there she was. There were many pictures of Tilly, smiling in front of paintings and sculptures. There was even one of her wearing the same tunic she'd been wearing the first time Lara met her. That one had been taken a few months before, in Spain, in an article about a large community art project. Tilly was holding a suspiciously clean paint brush and laughing. There was another of the same project where the main artist was in the foreground and Tilly, in paint spattered shorts and t-shirt was in the background, frowning as she concentrated on her work. Lara zoomed in on the photograph. Tilly was so beautiful. So much fun. And Lara was so in love with her.

The thought made her fingers freeze mid zoom. Was that true? Was she in love with Tilly? Everything rational in her screamed that she couldn't possibly be. They'd known each other for less than three days. How can you fall in love with someone in three days? You can't. But in those three days, they'd spent so much time together. It was weeks, months, concentrated into mere hours. Tilly had seen her angry, sad and happy. She'd held her gently, kindly before she'd held her with need and passion. If she could feel so close to her in just a matter of days, imagine how she'd feel if she'd known her for a whole week. A whole month? Imagine a whole year!

Lara looked back at the picture on the screen. Had she been too hasty walking away? After all, what was waiting for her back home? It was Boxing Day now. Nothing would have changed. Her flat would be empty and lifeless. Sure, she'd have her own clothes and her own shower... but really, was it better than more days spent with Tilly?

She had paused her fighting the world in order to let Tilly into her life. Why wasn't she taking up the fight to keep her in it?

Lara took a deep breath. No. She wasn't going to give up that easily. Tilly thought she didn't do commitment, but it was only because she was scared. Lara was scared too, but dammit, she wasn't going to let the fear win. She had always fought through the fear to get what she wanted. She wasn't about to stop now.

She opened a new browser and looked up train timetables. If she got off at the next station and got on a train going back up North, with a couple of changes, she could be back in Trewton Royd by tea time.

BY THE TIME SHE CAUGHT her connection, Tilly was feeling less optimistic. What if Lara's company refused to pass on her messages? Or worse, if they were closed until the New Year and she had to leave a message. She couldn't stay in London for ever, waiting for them to reopen. She supposed she could always head home. Wantage wasn't far from London.

What if she found Lara, but Lara didn't want to know her anymore? She had been very clear about not having time for a relationship right now. In fact, Tilly herself had said much the same. Staying in one place had never had any attraction to her before. But Lara... more time with Lara would be worth giving up on the travelling.

It was starting to snow again. The train drew to a halt. A few people stood up to get off. Tilly's gaze settled on the platform opposite where two people were standing, huddled into their coats as they waited for the train going in the opposite direction. One of them, a woman, was wearing a ridiculous coat that was clearly not meant for the weather. The same coat at Lara's. The woman looked up. Holy crap. Lara.

Tilly jumped up, grabbed her coat and bag. "Excuse me," she said and shuffled quickly out of her seat. People were boarding the train now and she had to push past them to get to the door before it closed. "Sorry. Sorry." She shouldered her way past and jumped out.

Standing on the platform, she couldn't see the woman on the other side anymore. Doubt crept in. What if it wasn't Lara? Had she just jumped off the train for nothing?

If it wasn't, she would just catch the next train and carry on with her journey. But if it was...

The whistle blew and the train pulled off. Tilly's heart hammered in her ears as she waited for it to leave, so that she could see. The train passed and the woman on the other platform was still there. Thank goodness.

"Lara!"

The woman on the other platform didn't hear. She looked up with line and seemed to perk up. Shit. Her train was coming. Tilly ran to the overhead bridge. "Lara. Wait."

She pounded up the steps, dodging past the stragglers from the crowd who had just got off the train. Across the bridge. The other train pulled into the station. Down the other side. The train doors opened. "Lara."

The other woman stepped onto the train.

Her heart was trying to wrench itself out of her chest. She stopped, panting and shouted, all the desperation of her soul in her voice. "Lara!"

A head popped out of the open train door. Lara.

Tilly whipped off her hat, and waved.

Hesitantly, Lara got off the train. The whistle blew. Lara stepped back, safely onto the platform. She stared at Tilly, her face seemingly frozen in shock. The train pulled out.

People brushed past Tilly, who was still standing there, panting. Her hand pressed against her racing heart.

As people dispersed, Lara walked towards her. "Tilly?"

"Lara, I'm sorry. Please give me another chance. I was stupid to say what I did. I want-"

Lara touched her face. "Why are you here?"

The tenderness in her voice was a little explosion of warmth in Tilly's chest. "I was taking the train to London to find you."

"You don't know where I live." A smile tugged at the corner of Lara's mouth. Her fingertip stroked Tilly's cheek, leaving a trail of delicious warmth. "Or have my phone number."

"I was going to see if your company would tell me how to get in touch. I know it's Christmas but..." Tilly said. "It's kind of a crazy plan, to be honest. But I was desperate."

Snowflakes drifted down. One settled on Tilly's eyelashes, making her blink. "I really like you, Lara," she said. "More than I've liked anyone in a long, long time. When I'm with you, the world feels different. It's like being with you has changed my place in it. You make me feel ... redefined." She gestured with her hands, as she tried to put the intensity of her feelings across. "When you left, I realised that ... love like that doesn't come along every day and you need to hold onto it. I was an idiot to let you go. I'll come to London with you. Or where ever. If you'll have me."

Lara's smile burst into being. "Tilly." She pulled her closer and kissed her, her mouth hot after the freezing air.

"Is that a yes, then?" said Tilly. Her heart was still galloping, but it was no longer from exertion.

"I think so," said Lara. She looked up at the timetable display screen. "Since there isn't another train for another forty minutes, why don't we go get a hot chocolate?"

"Excellent idea," said Tilly. They both started walking towards the station concourse. "And you can tell me why you were about to get on a train heading back up North."

"Isn't it obvious?" Lara grinned. "I was coming back to you."

And Tilly thought her heart would explode with happiness.

Chapter 12

Tilly looked at her phone and pulled a face. Lara nudged her. "Go on. You have to anyway, may as well get it over with."

They were sitting in Lara's living room, glasses of wine and crisps on the table. Since Lara had almost no decorations, Tilly had gone to Poundland and got a few bits to make a small wood and paper Christmas tree to go on her coffee table. It looked tasteful, but a little lonely set against Lara's sparse furnishings.

Tilly was meant to be calling her parents. It was the 29th now and she had spent the last three days in a haze of happiness. Unlike their time in Trewton Royd, being in Lara's flat felt more real. More grounded. She had been impressed how grown up Lara's life seemed, while Lara, who didn't seem to be able to cook anything beyond cheese on toast, was completely wowed by Tilly's limited repertoire of dishes.

This was nice. She could get used to it.

Tilly glanced across at Lara, who raised her eyebrows.

"The sooner you get it done..." said Lara.

"Do you want to come with me?" Tilly said, suddenly.

"We've only been together a week. Are you sure you want me to meet your parents?" Lara took a sip of wine. "Seems a bit sudden."

Tilly considered it. "No. You've already met Vinnie and Tracey. Meeting mum and dad will be okay, I should think."

Lara took another gulp of wine. "If you're sure."

Tilly leaned across and put her finger under Lara's chin. She kissed her. "I'm sure," she said.

Lara smiled. "Me too."

"Okay then." Tilly scrolled through to her parent's number and hit call.

"Thilini!" Amma said, when she answered. "How are you darling?"

"I'm fine, Amma. I'm ... looking forward to seeing you."

"Oh good," said Amma. "You're still coming."

"Of course I am. I thought tomorrow lunchtime. Is that okay?"

"Excellent. I'll make chicken pilau for you. I know you like that."

She really did. "Actually, Amma. I was wondering... can I bring someone?"

There was a tiny gasp at the other end of the line. "Is it the girl that you met at Christmas?" her mother said. "The one from London?"

"Yes..." Lara said, warily. She didn't have to ask how her mother knew. Vinnie was such a gossip. "Is it okay if she comes?"

"Oh course it is!" Amma said. "Poor girl, she shouldn't be alone at New Year. Bring her. I'd love to meet her. Oh. I'll have to make up an extra bed. Thank goodness Arun and the kids are only coming for the day, otherwise I'd have to have the children sleeping in the bath. Does she like chicken pilau? Is there anything you'd like me to make for her?"

Tilly closed her eyes and let Amma's excitement wash over her. Vinnie had been right. Her mother was more worried about her lack of stability than her lack of convention. She opened her eyes to see find Lara staring quizzically at her.

"Um..." Tilly put her hand over the mouthpiece. "Mum says, is there anything you want her to make? Or is there anything you don't eat?"

"Citrus fruit brings me out in a rash, but otherwise, I'm good," said Lara, looking bemused.

Tilly conveyed the information. She chatted a bit more and finally hung up. She couldn't stop smiling.

"So, I take it that went well?" said Lara.

"Yeah. My mum is delighted that you're coming. I expect she'll try to feed you to within an inch of your life," said Tilly.

Lara looked at her glass. "My mum liked to feed people. It's an Asian hospitality thing, right?"

"Probably," said Tilly. She leaned forward and kissed Lara's cheek. "Thank you."

"For what?"

"For this." Tilly indicated the two of them. "And for agreeing to come home with me. Amma sounded so excited."

Lara blinked. "I like it that you have an Amma," she said. "Mine was a Mama."

Tilly put down her glass and took Lara's hands. She didn't know what to say, so she didn't say anything, just gave Lara's fingers a gentle squeeze.

Lara looked down at their joined hands and blinked hard. "My mama," she said, her voice shaking. "My mama would have liked you. I don't know how she would have felt about us... but she would have liked you. As a person."

Tilly got up and moved closer to Lara so that she could hug her. "I'm glad," she said into Lara's hair. "It means a lot to me."

Lara sniffed. "Me too," she said and hugged Tilly back.

They held each other for a few minutes. Lara sighed into Tilly's shoulder. "What are we going to do afterwards?" she whispered.

Tilly breathed in slowly. She had been trying not to think about that. These last few days with Lara had been a revelation. The urge to leave still popped up, but then she would remember the emptiness she'd felt watching the car taking Lara out of Trewton Royd and know that leaving was never going to be the right answer. The world was out of kilter without Lara. But they couldn't live in this haze of happiness forever. Soon Lara would have to go back to work and Tilly would be the annoying distraction that kept her from giving her all to the company. And Tilly wasn't sure how she felt about being tied to London. On the one hand, Lara was here. On the other ... she didn't know anyone in London and she was fairly sure she wouldn't fit in with the mainstream art scene. It would take her ages to find a place.

"I have to go back to work in a few days," said Lara. "You can live here, you're more than welcome, but that's a huge thing to ask." She sat back. "I can't ask you to give up being who you are. I don't want to be the woman who tied you down and ruined your fun."

Tilly nodded, thoughtfully. The fact that Lara was thinking the same things as she was had to mean that they were meant to be. The plan that had been sitting in the back of her mind came to the fore. "There's something ..." she said. "It's not ideal. But this friend of mine has a project based up north that needs a sculptor." Her heart sped up in her chest. This really was a big step. Bigger than she'd fully appreciated. "I know it's not on your doorstep, but we could talk to each other every day and we could come to see each other at weekends."

She watched Lara's face as the implications of this filtered through. "I could come to you once a fortnight," Lara said.

Tilly nodded. "Unless you had a client meeting or something."

A smile spread slowly across Lara's face. "And you could come here in the intervening weekends .... unless you were immersed in critical part of your project." Lara squeezed Tilly's hands.

"Exactly. This way, we'd both be able to have some space to focus on our work when we needed to and still see each other."

"Tilly!" Lara pulled her closer and kissed her. "It's the perfect solution."

It was a few moments before they let go of each other.

The fact that Lara understood made Tilly giddy with relief. She pushed a strand of hair behind her ear. "I have to check the position is still open."

"When can you find out?"

"Well, I could call her now." She reached across to her phone, which she had abandoned at the other end of the sofa.

Lara nodded. "I'll just go wash my face. Give you a bit of privacy." She nodded, almost to herself, and left the room.

Tilly scrolled through her contacts and found Diane's number.

"Tilly!" said Diane. "Merry Christmas, matey!" Her voice slurred a little.

"Have you been drinking already?" Tilly laughed. "It's only six o'clock."

"Haven't stopped since last night," said Diane, giggling.

"Look, er, this is probably a bad time." Tilly hadn't anticipated that Diane might not be in a fit state to talk to her about something serious. She bit her lip.

Diane cleared her throat. "Is something wrong?" she said, sounding suddenly sober. Tilly had forgotten how Diane could do that. She could let herself get tipsy on half a glass and be giddy but could also sober up in a snap.

"No. No. Nothing wrong," said Tilly. "It's about that offer to come join your project."

"Oh yes?" Now her voice was sharp with interest. "Have you decided?"

"I'd like to accept. If the offer is still open."

Diane whooped. "Of course it's still open! That's fantastic! I'll email you the paperwork when ... er ... Probably in the New Year, to be honest. That's the best present you could have given me! Brilliant!"

"You won't say that when I'm in your way all the time!" Tilly laughed. She spoke to Diane for a minute or so more and hung up.

Lara was standing by the door, looking worried.

Tilly grinned. "I'm in," she said.

Lara beamed. "That is such a great solution. I was so worried about how I would fit work around a proper relationship. I felt terrible worrying about it. I thought you'd be upset."

"I know I can't compete with Haulistic Solutions," Tilly said. "I would be stupid to try."

"I love that you understand that. I'm so lucky to have found you."

"Yeah," said Tilly. "You so are."

NEW YEAR'S EVE ARRIVED and Lara found herself outside Tilly's parents' house. Tilly took her hand and they approached the front door together. When Tilly rang the doorbell, the door was flung open by a chubby Asian lady, who was unmistakably Tilly's mother.

"Darling!"

Tilly was pulled straight into a hug.

"Let me look at you. You've got so thin. Have you not been eating? How are you?" Another hug. It couldn't have been more different to the polite welcome she got when she went to see her dad and stepmother. Lara watched and suddenly felt awash with envy. How could Tilly not want to come home, when coming home meant this much love?

"Amma, this is Lara." Tilly gestured, her expression wary.

Lara stepped forward. There was a moment of quiet at the two women studied each other. Remembering her manners, Lara said, "Nice to meet you, aunty."

Tilly's mum smiled. "Lara," she said, warmly. "Welcome to our home." She touched her arm, gently. "Come, can I get you a tea? Something to eat? I've made gingerbread. And cinnamon and raisin cookies, of course." She rolled her eyes. "They're Vinnie's favourite. I have to make those. Come. Come. You must be exhausted after your journey."

They were ushered, not into the living room, but into a kitchen, where the dining table had been set with a variety of biscuits and cakes.

Tracey was already there, nursing a mug and chatting to Tilly's father. More introductions followed. Tilly's father beamed at her. "I hear you've decided to go out with this reprobate," he said, patting Tilly's shoulder fondly. "If you can keep her in one place for more than ten minutes, you are more than welcome to join this family!"

"Appachi!" said Tilly, her cheeks flaming. "I'm sorry about my family, Lara."

Lara laughed. "It's fine," she said. It really was.

"As it happens," Tilly said. "I've got some news. Do you remember my friend Diane?"

"Of yes, how is she? Isn't she getting married soon?" said Amma.

"Yes, next year," said Tilly.

Lara tried not to laugh as Tilly's announcement was derailed by her mother bombarding her with questions about Diane's wedding.

Tilly looked exasperated. "As I was saying," she said firmly. "Diane's got a project in the north, and they need a sculptor. She's offered it to me and I've accepted." She grinned. "Which means I'll be in the UK for the next eighteen months as least." She reached for Lara's hand. "Hopefully, longer." The look she gave her was so full of love and hope that Lara felt her knees go weak.

"Oh, that's wonderful!" Tilly's mother clasped her hands together and her father beamed.

"Well, we have even more to celebrate, then," he said. "If this is your doing, we'll definitely keep you," he said to Lara.

"I don't intend to let her go," said Tilly. They sat down at the table together.

The kettle boiled and Lara's mother made tea. Vinnie arrived with a couple of shopping bags and there was a fresh round of greetings. Amma told him the news.

"Excellent! You took it." He came over and put his arms around both of them to give them a hug. To her surprise, Lara didn't feel awkward. The hug felt like another layer of acceptance. Vinnie grabbed a cinnamon and raisin biscuit and went over to sit next to Tracey.

"Wait a minute, you knew about this project?" said his mother. "And you didn't tell me?"

Lara laughed at Vinnie's guilty expression. She sipped her mug of tea as the conversation rose and fell around her. If Trewton had felt like a community, this was even better. She watched Tilly, sitting next to her, fending off her family's questions and couldn't stop the smile that spread across her face. There was no doubting the way she felt about this woman. A future with her was a challenge and a joy at the same time. Lara grinned. Finally, she was home.

They both were.

The End

THANK YOU FOR READING *Christmas for Commitment-phobes*. If you enjoyed it, please leave a review at your favourite book retailer. It doesn't need to be long – just a quick couple of lines will do.

Thank you, thank you, thank you in advance!

Rhoda

WHAT TO READ NEXT

If you enjoyed *Christmas for Commitmentphobes* why not try the rest of the Trewton Royd series. They can all be read as standalone stories:

Snowed In – Exhausted tech millionaire Tracey wants time to recharge. Vinnie wants to lick his wounds, alone. Being trapped together in a snowstorm is the last thing either of them needs.

Belonging – Harriet is still grieving when her late lover's teenage daughter turns up on her doorstep. Can helping the teenager move on help Harriet too?

That Holiday in France – Just when Ellie decides she doesn't need a man to complete her, she meets Ash. But does she like him enough to give up her independence?

Want a free Christmas novella?

Join my newsletter and get a Christmas novella absolutely free.

-BRITISH-ASIAN HEROINE

-plus sized hero

-set in a microbiology lab

-Christmas

TO GET YOUR FREE COPY go to my website www.rhodabaxter.com[1], where a sign up link is available.

---

1. http://www.rhodabaxter.com

Preview of chapter 1 of That Holiday in France.

That Holiday in France
Rhoda Baxter

A*pril*

Ellie was late getting home because of the rain. She shook her umbrella out on the doorstep, and rushed in to put it in the kitchen sink before it dripped everywhere.

"That you, our Ellie?" her dad said, from the living room.

"Yes, it's me." She took off her coat and hung it up.

"What've you got for us today?"

She popped her head round the door to find her dad sitting in his chair, still in his work overalls but without his shoes, with the telly on low. "How was work?" she asked him.

He shrugged. "Same as ever. How about you? How's the cakes?"

"Not bad," she said. "I've got some apricot tarts and a few bits of fruit cake."

His eyes crinkled into a hint of a smile. "Ah. Lovely."

"Do you want another cuppa to go with it?"

He nodded, drained his mug and held it out to her.

Ellie went into the living room to take it from him. Close up, he looked tired and, to Ellie's surprise, old.

Back in the kitchen she frowned as she made the tea. Strong tea, two sugars for Dad. Milky tea, one sugar for her.

She popped two of the apricot tarts and the crumbling cake on a plate. The best perk from working in the bakery was that she got to take home some of the cakes that were too wonky or broken to sell. She saved the least damaged apricot tart to give to Luke.

She looked at the clock. Oh no. Later than she'd thought.

She rushed through, two mugs clutched in one hand, the plate with the cakes in the other. She pushed the door open with her bum and backed in.

"Here you go, dad." She put his mug down on the side table next to him, nudging the remote control out of the way.

"Ah, you're a good gel," he said. He picked up a tart and examined it. It had an apricot half embedded in frangipane. The cakes in the shop had a delicate glaze over the top. Being a reject, this particular tart had singed a little on the top. "This looks fancy."

"It's Sue's new recipe," she said. "I've not tried it yet." She grabbed her own and said, "I can't stay down here and chat, dad. Luke's coming over in a bit to pick me up. I'd better get ready."

He looked disappointed, but nodded. "There's some post for you. Nice, posh looking envelope." He nodded towards the windowsill, where the post usually ended up. The days were lengthening, so the curtains were still open. When her mother had been around, the curtains were drawn and the lights were on by now.

Ellie stifled a sigh and put her tart back on the plate. She turned on the lights, rescued the post and drew the curtains. The net curtain was looking a little grey. She'd have to wash them again soon, once it stopped raining quite so much. She looked down at the post. The envelope was creamy and thick. "That is fancy," she said, quietly.

"You going to open it, then?"

She sank down onto the small two seater sofa and opened it, trying not to tear too much. The postmark was foreign. For one insane second, she thought maybe Mum was writing to her.

"Oh, hurry up, lass," her father said. He was clutching his mug of tea and leaning forward.

She winced at the lovely paper tore at the end and pulled out a card. A wedding invitation. She opened it and quickly scanned what was inside. "Oh my god!" She giggled and put her hand over her mouth. "You'll never guess what, dad. You remember Sophie from school? She's getting married."

"Oh aye." He leaned back again, and brought his tea up to his face to blow on it. "What's she doing now? Went somewhere down south didn't she?"

"She went to university," Ellie said. She herself had stopped going to school at seventeen and taken on more hours at Sue's bakery. She didn't regret it, mind, but sometimes she wondered what it must be like to leave Trewton Royd and go somewhere else. Most of her friends who had left had drifted away, out of her orbit, but Sophie had stayed in touch. "She got a job in France last summer and stayed there."

"Who's she marrying then?" her father said. "Anyone we know?"

"Ethan. She met him at university." Ethan was tall and handsome and French. Hence Sophie's move to France.

There was a note written on the inside of the invitation. 'Ellie, I know it's a long way, but I hope you can come. There will be a few people from Trewton there, but not many. Ethan's grandparents have this fabulous old place. If you RSVP before the end of next month, I can try and save a room for you and Luke. If not, there's also lots of space to pitch a tent in the garden. I really hope you can be there. Love Sophie'.

"Aww," she said. "She's getting married in France. How exciting."

Her father sniffed. "Shame you won't be able to go," he said. "Bit rude that, sending you an invite knowing you can't come. Rubbing your face in it."

"What?" She looked up. "Who says I'm not going?"

"Well y'aren't are ye?" he said. "It's bloody expensive and it's all the way in that Europe. We're trying to get out from under bloody Europe. We don't need to be travelling across to France, swelling their coffers." He turned his face back to the telly. "Bloody Europe. Bloody Europeans."

Ellie sighed. This again. "It's been ten years," she said. "And I'm not Mum."

No response. "I'll have Luke with me, anyway."

"Didn't stop your mum, did it?" It was a growl.

Ellie opened her mouth to argue and then shut it. What was there to say? They had gone on holiday and while Dad slept off his hangover, Mum had met Arno and fallen in love. It had taken another two years of furtive calls and meetings before she left, but Dad had never trusted anything European since. Or women. She put the card carefully back into the envelope. "I'll talk to Luke and see what he thinks."

"You do that," said her father. "He'll tell you the same as me. You'll see."

Ellie tucked the envelope into her waistband, grabbed her tea and the plate which now only had one pastry on it and made for the door. "If you need me," she said. "I'll be upstairs getting ready."

LUKE, WHEN HE ARRIVED, wasn't impressed with the invitation. "Oh, she's getting married in France, is she? What's wrong with Yorkshire? Not good enough for her?"

"I dunno, I think it sounds nice, having a wedding in France." Ellie had never been to France. Dad had refused to let her go on the school's French exchange trip. She thought of the family she'd seen on *Location, Location, Location*, who had all moved to a French chateau. "I think it sounds dead romantic." She put the envelope carefully back on her bedside table.

Luke rolled his eyes. "I didn't know you were even in touch with Sophie."

"She's my best friend!"

"Was, love. Was. She's barely looked at any of us since she went off to uni." Luke stood and looked at his watch. Clearly, it was time to go.

"We go out for a drink every time she comes home." She realised how defensive she sounded. Sophie didn't come home often, it was true. But she did email a couple of times a week at least, and when they met up, it took a few minutes for them to catch up, and the months fell away. "We talk to each other a lot, thanks."

"Course you do." Luke gave Ellie an affectionate pat on the bottom before clattering down the stairs. He popped his head into the living room. "We'll be off now, Roy," he said to Ellie's dad.

"Have a good time," Dad said.

When Ellie joined Luke, her father said, "See you later, then, love."

They set off in the balmy evening to walk to the pub. It was quiz night. Ellie put her hands in the pockets of her denim jacket. Luke gently teased one of her hands out and curled his big, warm hand around it.

"I know it'd be nice to go to Sophie's do," he said. "But face it, babe, we can't afford to go to France, even if we wanted to. We're saving up, remember. For when we move in together."

"Yes, I know, but maybe we could -"

"You want to spend money that we're saving so that we can start our own future, to go to someone else's wedding?" said Luke. "Don't be daft." He tucked her hand into his arm and strode on.

Ellie hurried along, to keep up. Their future. Everyone talked about it as though it was a done deal. She and Luke had been together for nearly four years, since she was seventeen, and they were going to get married. Fact. Except Luke hadn't actually asked her to marry him ... or even to move in with him.

"Luke," she said, as they got to the end of the main road that wound its way down towards the village. "You know you haven't asked me yet."

"Asked you what?"

"To move in with you. You've just assumed we would."

He stopped walking and turned to face her. "We talked about it. I don't have to propose. It's not like getting married."

"I don't think we did discuss it," said Ellie. "You just said."

"Ellie," said Luke. "What are you trying to say? Do you not want to move in with me? Is that what this is about?"

She looked at him, at his eyes which were narrowed in annoyance, at his scowl. He wasn't very nice when he looked like that. He was much bigger than she was. When they'd first got together, she had loved the way he stood protectively by her. Now, just sometimes, she wasn't so sure what he was protecting her from.

"Well?" he said. "Because if that's what you're saying, we may as well not bother with any of this." He shook her hand out from the crook of his arm and stepped closer. "What are we doing going out together if we don't move in together? Where's the future in that?" He was very close. She fought the urge to step back.

She shook her head. "That's not what I meant," she said. "Forget I said anything, it's all fine."

"Is all this fuss because I said you can't go to that wedding in France?"

"No, it's fine. Let's go. We need to get to the pub before the quiz starts." She started off again, he paused for a beat before following her.

THE PUB WAS BUSY, LIKE it always was on quiz night. The 'team', mostly men from the garage where Luke worked, were sitting in their favourite place - at a table by the quiz machine. Sometimes, one of the girlfriends came too, but not tonight. Luke went to get the drinks in, leaving Ellie to say hello to the guys. Someone had just finished a packet of peanuts. Ellie looked at it. "You know," she said. "I really fancy some peanuts." She got back to her feet. "Anyone else?" she asked.

"Get us another packet of ready salted, would you Ellie," one of the guys said.

When she got to the bar, Luke said, "Is something wrong?"

"No. Just fancied some peanuts." She smiled at Phil, the landlord. "Hiyya Phil. Can I have two packets of peanuts please - ready salted."

Phil passed her two packs and returned his attention to the pint he was pulling for Luke. Ellie passed some money to Luke, picked up the peanuts and turned to go.

"I've ordered us chips," Luke said.

"Lovely." They always had chips on quiz night. It served as a meal until they went back to hers, when she would make them late night cheese on toast before they went to bed. As she made her way back to the table, she wished Sophie were there. She liked Luke's friends, but there wasn't much that she could talk to them about. No one 'got' her like Sophie did.

Someone called her name. Ellie turned. A young man jumped up from his seat at a table not far away. He was thin, tall and brown skinned. "Hi Ellie."

She smiled. "Ash! Hiyya. How're you? How's uni?"

"Good. Good, thank you." He pushed his black hair back from his forehead.

"You're looking well," she said. He looked different since the last time she'd seen him. He seemed to have grown taller, and he was certainly more outgoing than he used to be. This time last year, he would barely have spoken more than a few words to her. Even that would have been at a mumble. "I almost didn't recognise you just now."

"Thanks, I think," he said, giving her a friendly smile. "I ... er ... did you hear from Sophie? About the wedding?"

"Oh yes, isn't it brilliant. A wedding in France sounds so exotic." She remembered that Sophie knew Ash quite well. They'd had some classes together. Physics or something.

He nodded, put his hands in his pockets and bounced a little on the balls of his feet. "Are you … are you going?"

"Ah, no. Probably not."

"Oh?" He looked surprised. "Why not? Since you guys were friends, I thought …"

Well yes. You would think she'd be going to her best friend's wedding. Ellie forced herself to smile. "Well, Luke-"

"Did someone mention my name?" Luke appeared beside her and put his arm around her. "Alright, Ass?"

Ellie winced.

Ash stilled at the old school nickname, and took his hands out of his pockets. "Luke."

"What are you two gossiping about?" said Luke, giving Ellie's shoulders a squeeze.

"Ash," Ellie said, pointedly, "was just asking if I was going to Sophie's wedding."

"Oh, she's not," said Luke.

Ash looked at Ellie, a question in his frown.

"Can't afford it," she said, quickly. "It's a shame, really. I'd have loved to go."

"You're going, I suppose," said Luke.

"I was thinking about it, yes." Ash's gaze moved from Luke, to the arm holding Ellie firmly and back to Luke. Suddenly, Ellie felt very small.

"I suppose you'll be dipping into your trust fund," Luke sneered.

Ash's eyes flicked upwards. "I don't have a trust fund."

"Yes, well it's okay for your sort," said Luke cryptically.

Ellie knew that Ash wasn't rich. He worked in the corner shop in the holidays. She had only spoken to him a few times, when she went to deliver the bread to the shop, and he seemed like a nice guy. She didn't know why Luke was being so weird. She gave Luke a quizzical look, which he ignored.

"Anyway, come on, love. Let's go sit down, shall we?" Luke steered her away.

She mouthed 'sorry' to Ash as she was led away. He raised a hand, as though to say it was fine.

"Did you have to be so rude?" she said to Luke.

"Well, he was hitting on my girl, so yes. He's lucky I didn't do worse."

"We were having a conversation. He was not hitting on me. He was asking me if I was going to my friend's wedding. Which I really should be."

Luke stopped and frowned. "What has got into you today, Ellie?"

For a second she was speechless. She fought to think of a response that wasn't just a wail of 'I want to go to Sophie's wedding'.

"Anyways," said Luke. "Looks like the quiz is starting."

And just like that, she missed her chance. Ellie sat down, threw one packet of peanuts across to the man who'd wanted them and tore open her own. Someone passed her the pen and paper with 'you've got the best handwriting'. She took it and bent her head so that no one could see her fume.

This is the end of the sample chapter. To continue reading, buy That Holiday In France now!

That Holiday in France

When Ellie's boyfriend forbids her from going to France to attend her best friend's wedding, she decides she's had enough. She dumps him and goes to France by herself. But travelling alone is scary and Ellie realises how reliant she'd become on the men in her life.

On holiday, she learns to trust her own judgement and grows in confidence. Just when she decides she doesn't need a man to complete her, she meets Ash, who is everything her ex wasn't.

But is Ellie willing to give up her new found independence and link herself to another man?

* Friends to lovers
* Heroine asserting her independence
* Summer in France
* Tiny puddings

That Holiday In France is a standalone story set in the little Yorkshire village of Trewton Royd. Ideal for fans of Mhairi McFarlane or Sophie Kinsella.

Other Books by Rhoda Baxter

Trewton Royd small town romance novellas - All can be read as standalone stories

PAT'S PANTRY - short story

SNOWED IN

BELONGING

CHRISTMAS FOR COMMITMENTPHOBES

THAT HOLIDAY IN FRANCE

SMART GIRLS SERIES -All can be read as standalone stories

GIRL ON THE RUN – nominated for Joan Hessayon award

GIRL HAVING A BALL - nominated for Romantic Comedy of the Year 2017 RoNA awards

GIRL IN TROUBLE

GIRL AT CHRISTMAS - novella

Short Stories

KISSCHASE - A collection of six short stories

THE TRUTH ABOUT THE OTHER GUY

ONE NIGHT IN SHINING ARMOUR

Books Written as Jeevani Charika

CHRISTMAS AT THE PALACE – shortlisted for the Emma prize and The Pink Heart Soc reader choice

THIS STOLEN LIFE – Longlisted for Guardian Not The Booker Prize

A CONVENIENT MARRIAGE – shortlisted for RoNA contemporary romantic novel award 2020

About the Author

Rhoda Baxter writes contemporary romances with heart and a touch of cynicism. She also writes a Jeevani Charika. Her books have been shortlisted for awards such as the RoNA Romantic Comedy of the Year (in 2017), Love Stories Award (in 2015) and the Joan Hessayon Award (2012).

Rhoda started off as a microbiologist and then drifted out of research and into technology transfer. When choosing a penname, she was hit by a fit of nostalgia and named herself after the bacterium she studied during her PhD.

She has lived in a variety of places including Sri Lanka, Yap (it's a real place), Halifax, Oxford and Didcot (also a real place). She now lives with her young family in East Yorkshire, where there are enough tea shops to keep her happy.

You can find her wittering on about cake and science and other random things on her website (http://www.rhodabaxter.com), on Facebook[1], or on Twitter (@rhodabaxter). Please do say hello if you're passing.

You can also follow her on Bookbub[2].

Don't forget, you can get a free copy of one of her books by joining her reader newsletter[3].

---

1.   https://en-gb.facebook.com/RhodaBaxterAuthor/

2.   https://www.bookbub.com/authors/rhoda-baxter

3.   https://www.subscribepage.com/CforC

www.rhodabaxter.com